HOE #999:
Decennial Appreciation
and Celebratory Analysis

or

The Dead Un-Dead

HOE #999:
Decennial Appreciation and Celebratory Analysis

or

The Dead Un-Dead

Jarett Kobek

Semina No. 6

What is commonest and cheapest and nearest and easiest is Me
—Walt Whitman, 1855

One:
You Wanted the Best

The Proposal

Necessary Background

Prior to mass consumerist engagement with the Internet, individualised electronic communications occurred via privately-owned-and-operated Bulletin Board Systems. These crude mechanisms grew into hyper-specific colonies of outsider culture, many intersecting with the pseudo-nihilistic ethos of DIY/punk. These outposts created their own medium — a stripped down and denuded version of paper zines known as 'textfiles' or 'e-zines'.

My personal engagement with textfiles began at age thirteen. Writing under the *nom de guerre* of Squinky, I crafted an adolescent body of absurdist texts that embarrass me to the present day. After discovering sex, I fell away from the scene only to be re-engaged in the post-Internet late nineties by the group known as HOE (Hogs of Entropy).

A self-consciously Dadaist experiment, HOE practised deliberate stupidity in an archaic artform enveloped within the more flexible and monetisable medium of the Web. HOE files were often incomprehensible and intentional garbage, but the group attracted writers with backgrounds who had never been embraced by the textfiles scene. Roughly 1,100 files saw release.

Personally, HOE became a place to practise a Whitman-by-way-of-Kathy Acker-esque shamanistic summoning and demonic exorcism. Under the newly adopted pseudonym of AIDS, my work culminated in *HOE #999, The Madcap Laughs*, a text that I would argue is possibly the most artistically significant achievement of the entire scene—an obscenely explicit overview and crude invocation of *fin-de-siècle* America seen from the pre-9/11 daze of Rudy Giuliani's New York and filtered through a poetic dialectic of dotcom-era technobabble.

The Set-Up

HOE #999 continues to haunt the Internet, semi-pirated on retro-computing nostalgia sites and utterly stripped of its original context. The year 2010 is the decennial anniversary of the file's release, and in light of this milestone, I propose a rescue operation of my work through a perverse transformation of the text from its electronic origins into an expanded paper format, conjoined with a scholarly apparatus that makes apparent my original intent.

To achieve this, I suggest a novel in three parts:

1. Scholarly Apparatus—Using my own funds, and under the pretext that I have been invited to provide a personal overview of my textfiles to a small gallery specialising in contemporary art, I will outsource the writing of a 10,000 word critical essay on *HOE #999* to a Subcontinental Asian essay farm. These businesses operate as literary sweatshops, relying on India and Pakistan's plethora of overeducated and underemployed college graduates to ghost-write technical manuals, blog posts and other sundry works for the West.

The proposed essay will be structured and informed by an outline that I will provide, and be written in the first person, as if by myself. As a work-for-hire enterprise, the final product will be, in every legal sense, mine.

2. Epistles and Documentary History — All documents regarding the project will be harvested and reprinted within the book. This includes not only communiqués with the essay farm — in which I will make brazenly clear the unethical aspects of my intent — but supplementary materials such as this proposal. By interspersing this aspect of the project throughout the overall text, a background narrative will drive the flow of the text with the most archaic of all novelistic forms — the Victorian epistolary.

I would also include some communication between myself and the *Semina* series' editors about the structure and nature of the book; this level of transparency will not only be instructive about the nature of the process, but, given the largely undocumented input from editors, would add another layer to the ambiguity of the project's final authorship.

3. Excerpts from *HOE #999* — The heart of the matter shall itself be sampled throughout the novel. *HOE #999* is roughly 20,000 words in length, providing ample material. While some content is impossible to present on paper, there are many fragments suitable for print publication. These will appear textually, if not visually, unaltered from their original appearance.

As may seem obvious, *HOE #999* is the anchor of the whole project — but it bears emphasis that this project will work at its most effective structured around a vaguely-lost work from my own history. Only by engaging with the personal — and marrying it to the apparently impersonal and unethical — can we achieve the confusion necessary for success.

(I reserve the right to revise and edit any sections of one and
two, and to acknowledge this within the text itself. Here we
twist the entire project back upon itself—a book apparently
written, in part, by anonymous workers from the Third World
may, in truth, be written by the person whose name is on the
frontispiece.)

Final Judgement

This project will inject consumer issues yet to fully infiltrate
publishing, one of the few product-driven industries
mostly untouched by the ethical concerns of globalisation.
Furthermore, by employing a literary worker from the Third
World, we will attack the very concept of authorial identity.
In providing at least four possible sources for the text—
Jarett Kobek, Squinky/AIDS, the *Semina* series' editors
and an unknown person of non-Caucasian, and thus foreign,
extraction—the rudderless reader will be complicit in our
conceit, mirroring the general collusion of consumers under
the yoke of G13 post-globalisation capitalism.

We destroy the illusion of literary exceptionalism.

```
    s$
    $$      .d""b. .d""b.              HOE E'ZINE #999
[-- $$""b.  $$  $$ $$  $$  -- ----------------------------------------- --]
    $$  $$ $$  $$ $$ $$ss$$            "THE MADCAP LAUGHS"
    $$  $$ $$  $$ $$ $$                       by AIDS
    $$  $$ $$  $$ $$ $$ $$                    1/09/00
[-- $$  $$ $$  $$ $$ $$ $$ -- ----------------------------------------- --]
    $$  $$ "TssT" "TssT"
```

          COUNT YONDER CLOCKS THAT TICK THE HANDS OF TIME
    tickety tockty sickity sockety slappery-doo sippery simperer sooie

    tired of all my lies being made public, he said, and I could only
nod in response. Had only someone told Mister Jarett Kobek that the
world was not prepared for those without a non-discloser policy, perhaps
the crucifixion would have happened later than sooner. There were 18
before Christ and 1 after, and the last was the last, and his name was
Kobek and the Pharisees and the Saducees did fear him as they feared God.
For they knew he was not of God, but something bigger.
    THE HONESTY POLICY: and he didn't mean that the divine unity and
st. sophia, ah st. sophia, he didn't mean that you gave out a thousand
little disbursements of the bawdy details of your life, no, that could
never be considered honesty, but rather a form of decadent self-deception;
no, the honesty he brought was that in your face ruthless persecution of
your human flaws. YOU THOUGHT YOU WERE IN LOVE but he told you it would
be over by next summer; and was he ever right? 1 + 3 = 4 times a lady.
What all the whores propound to have, but none really do. It's alright
to push it so far, push it so far up and in, but the cervix is the end; but
ah, this is why the Pharisees fled; he knew how to move INTO the cervix,
bringing cancer and death at both hands: AND BEHOLD I SAW DEATH AND HE
ROAD A PALE HORSE AND HELL FOLLOWED WITH HIM; verily, I did say, Here was
the edited version of the new testament, not that it necessarily means
anything to the likes of you:

    JOHN
    EPISTLES OF PAUL
    ACTS (with caveat introduction)

It ever shall be hard for you to kick against the pricks.

                      They burned brands of your heart
                             into cattle
                  in the heartland

Gavin Everall to Kobek — 8 July 2009

Dear Jarett,

We've just had a meeting with Stewart Home about the shortlist for the next and final round of *Semina* publications. While we did shortlist a total of six proposals, we all agreed your proposal was outstanding. So to move things on, especially as your proposal was quite ambitious, we'd like to offer you a commission for *HOE #999: Decennial Analysis and Celebratory Appreciation*. I hope that you are still interested in working with us and publishing in this series.

If you are happy to go ahead I'll get a contract mailed to you, and I'll also send copies of the first four books we've commissioned, which will give you an idea of the series' design. The contract details the schedule, but we'd normally request a draft by November.

It would also be good if we can meet. I'm in NY in October at the NY Art Book Fair, so perhaps we can arrange to meet up then? Unfortunately Stewart won't be there but if you were in London it would be good for you to meet up with him at some point, and perhaps particularly during the editing process. Let me know if this is possible.

If you are happy with this, I'll send a contract over.

Yours
Gavin Everall

On the Nature of Composition

Some people invent colours for each vowel. Others taste them. There are forms and rules for every consonant. There is a poetry recognised by all senses. The alchemy of composition, of vision reduced into words. The hope of capturing a totality of expression. Nothing lost, all said. Every iota wrung out and bottled. And then there are those who see weakness in the word, shuddering at the inherent incapacity of language. No name of a thing represents the thing. A third-hand glimpse impressed upon the consciousness of a stranger. No attempt can seize the world.

Much might be said for either side. But who wants the bother? Ideology of aesthetic expression is as dreadful as the classics. Fourierism, National Socialism, Maoism, veganism, polyamory. Yawn. The connecting thread is the linkage of lifestyle with zealotry. The paradox of an individual incapable of individuality resolved through the hive. Sex, diet, voting records and musical taste determine personality, carve out whole lives. You die for the word. Unless the word cannot encompass death. Then you die for its inefficacy.

But me?

I'm with the KLF: 'We await the day with relish that somebody dares to make a dance record that consists of nothing more than an electronically programmed bass drum beat that continues playing the fours monotonously for eight minutes. Then, when somebody else brings one out using exactly the same bass drum sound and at the same beats per minute (B.P.M.) we will all be able to tell which is the best, which inspires the dance floor to fill the fastest, which has the most sex and the most soul. There is no doubt, one will be better than the other. What we are basically saying is, if you have anything in you, anything unique, what others might term as originality, it will come through whatever the component parts used in your future Number One are made up of.'

This idea was the guiding ethos of *HOE #999*, a text crafted from component cultural units and writings spirited from sundry sources. One method was sampling of a few words from a random website and then copying several more from another. Eventually sentences were formed that became blocks of text. Sometimes coherent, often not. Another approach included the wholesale appropriation of materials in identifiable chunks. This says nothing of references to other works littered throughout. The project *HOE #999* was positioned chronologically at the bottom of 10,000 years. It is the waste-spigot-rectum of civilisation—the place where it all comes out. High, low and in-between.

Like a bass drum playing 4/4, a voice emerges. Mine. It was the Autumn and Winter of 1999. I thought of the visual and auditory arts, their natures of encompassment and I attempted to emulate their methods. I opened the floodgates and let it flow over me. All writing was mine to sample, all materials. I stole from the many and I stole from the few. I collided texts together. I transmitted the nonsense into sense. The method of creation ceased mattering once the monster came to life. I'd gone Victor von and created a thing. Each word was my own.

Consider a dense tapestry, woven together by various threads. Each strand might have a unique value—perhaps a richness of material. Yet the sum of individual values pales compared with the merit of collective interweaving. Different threads become one shimmering thing. A tapestry is more than a collection of its threads. Its value exceeds strings.

'An angry debate has erupted in France over the increasingly negative reviews being delivered to French films by local critics. As reported by a Paris-based correspondent for the London Sunday Times, the debate reached its peak last week when director Patrice Leconte proposed that negative reviews be banned until audiences have a chance to make up their own minds about new releases. In addition, a manifesto published by a group of French film devotees declared that French critics were experiencing a "crisis of intelligence and competence" and concluded: "We have everything to lose if the critics treat us this way, and the Americans have everything to gain." Critics shot back that if the filmmakers (who are largely state supported) made watchable films, they would not be attracting negative reviews. The debate occurred during a week when Disney's Tarzan set a record for the biggest opening-day take in French history. Commented the Sunday Times correspondent: "Given the choice of a Disney movie and a homegrown selection of dreary meditations on unhappy families and bad sex, French film-goers voted with their eyeballs".'

Bills for the Spring 2000 semester will be mailed beginning December 6, 1999. Please verify that your address is correct by checking on "Albert". This will ensure the receipt of your spring registration bill.

    PLEASE VERIFY THAT YOUR SOUL IS ON TOP OF THE SOUL MENDING GAME / I WON'T TAKE ANY BLAME / when I write poetry and I need to emphasize words, I have come upon the amazing idea / I will just capitalize my words / LIKE THIS / See? / Why did you have to come into MY BEDROOM at night, FATHER? / Why did you have to PENETRATE ME? / I was your LITTLE GIRL and you ABUSED me / I don't want to DIE tonight

                        LOOSE LIPS SINK SHIPS

    I always remember seeing the bumper sticker on the tractor and I wondered then and I wonder now if hirohito knew that I would drive it over him as I did. THE

    THE ACTUALITY OF YOUR OWN EXISTENCE: the secrets of their lives is S-E-sssh! FIVE WACKY PROLETARIAT ENGLISH IDIOTS! S-E-echz LIVING THE BIOSPHERE won't you come around here? Won't you blow your bubbles here? Saved saved we're all saved from something but was there ever a present danger in the first place? Lord, I don't know. THE SECRET OF THEIR LIVES IS S-E-X. I can smell the v.d. in the club tonight. You turn my heart on. Can't you feel it rhythmically beating to the pounding of my erection? PULSE PULSE BEAT BEAT I wanna come all over you BABY, and when I CUMMMMM, my CUMMMM will the the elixir of life that Ponce de Leon and Polly Jean Harvey sought for all of time. We've all become WILHEM REICH in our young age.. THE SECRETS OF THEIR LIVES IS S-E- Talk to me about all those men you were with, and oh, let's not forget all my ladies; now that we've discussed the pussy and the dick, which always are and always have been and always will be, now that we've discussed the ORGASM: we're all part of the club. THE HUMAN CIRCUS OF SEX. Yes, climb aboard. I know you need to talk to me about getting sucked off, JUST ONCE MORE; I know you need to tell me about how he fucks like a pimp, AGAIN AND AGAIN AND AGAIN. The

```
monotony of lust never ends... We keep it real. REAL STUPID. THE SECRET
OF THEIR LIVES IS S-E- hex. How many more times, God? How many more times
do I have to be in on the joke? The joke that is the merging of flesh
into some Aristophanic being. THE JOKE OF WHICH I'M ALWAYS THE PUNCH
LINE. I wish I could be a little less sensitive to the shit, but I can't.
The worst is how /boring/ it really is. I could see suffr'ing through it
all if it was interesting, if it was somehow funny, or anything, but it
isn't. It's over and done with. The joke has ceased to be amusing. You
can't impress or shock. I was fucking Grecian boys before you were a mote
in God's eye, and I was red socking their /legs/. What? Don't you get it?
Probably not.

     You're all amateurs. Remember that the next time you go to talk to
me about your multitudinous orgasms. You're bad at sex; you're an
amateur. And all the children cried on blackberry lane.

     In nomine Patris, et Filii, et Spiritus Sancti. Amen.
```

Years passed. Ten. I maintained an affection for *HOE* #999. It's got a certain quality. Now, as The Atrocity Exhibit gives me this space to celebrate my old work, I do hope you too will enjoy this fond friend from my past.

Kobek to The Hangman's Beautiful Daughter — 8 July 2009

<u>Memo from the Pleasure Dome:</u>

Fuck. So fucked. FUCK. They said yes. I have to do the *HOE* book. SO FUCKED.

'O, whistle, and I'll come to you, my lad'

```
"HAHAHAH REMEMBER WHEN YOU FUCKED THAT GIRL?"
'HAHAHAHA OH NO MAN HAHAHAH NO DON'T SAY THAT! NOT IN FRONT OF PEOPLE!"
"HAHAHAH REMEMBER HOW YOU SAID HER PUSSY WAS SHAPED LIKE A..."
"NO!!!!!"
"HAHAHAHAHAHAHA MAN WHY NOT?"
"HAHAHHAHAHAAHAHA CUZ MAN I DON'T WANT HER TO KNOW MAN! HAHAHAHA DON'T
```

SAY IT FRONT OF HER MAN! AHHAHAAH! BABY UH DON'T PAY ATTENTION BABY! HAHAHAH IT'S JUST YOU KNOW HAHAHA A SEX STORY! AHAHHAAH OH MY GOD SEX!!! 1HAHAHA IT'S FO FUNNY !!! JESUS CHRIST!!! MY DICK WAS IN HER MOUTh!!! HAHAHAHH OH MY GOD, BABY, MY DICK HAS BEEN IN YOUR MOUTH! HAHAHAHHAHAAH OH SHIT IT'S SO FUNNY AHAHAHAHA OH GOD I CAN'T STOP LAUGHING HAHAHAHAHA OH FUCK IT'S SEX HAHAHAHAHAHAHA OH SHIT SEX AHAHAHAHHAHAHAHA SEX HAHAHAHAHAHHAHA SEX AHAHAHAHAHHAHA SEX AHAHAHAHAHHAHA VAMPIRE BAT BITE SEX AHHAHAHAHAHAHA OH JESUS LORD IN HEAVEN ABOVE AHAHAHHAHAH SEX AHAHHAAHHA ORAL SEX AHHAHAHAHAHA DICK SUCKING HAHAHAHAHA PUSSY EATING HAHAHAHAHAH ANY SEXUAL EXPERIENCE IS THE VALIDATION FO THE FACT THAT I HAVE /SEEN/ THE DARK UNDERCURRENT OF LIFE HAHAHAHAHAHA OH GOD HAHAHHAHAHAHA I CAN'T STOP LAUGHING AHAHAHHA IT'S A PERFECT DAY.... FOR SEX!!!!! HAHAHAHAHAHA CAN'T YOU HEAR MY DRUM MACHINES BEATING TO THE RHYTHM OF SEX? AHHAHAHAHAHAHA OH GOD AND THEN I CAME HAHAHAHAHAHAH!!!! OH GOD!!! HAHAHAHAHA SEX!11! HAHAHAHAHA JESUS CHRIST SEX!!11 AHAHHAHAHAHAHAAH OH LORD IT'S SEX IT'S SEX CAN'T STOP LAUGHING ABOUT SEX!!! HAHAHAH ALOOOK! !!! IT'S SO SCANDALOUS THAT I SAID SEX!!! HAHAHAHA THAT'S FUNNY TOO!!1! WOW THE WHOLE HUMAN REPRODUCTIVE SYSTEM IS THE FUNNIEST JOKE I EVER HEARD!! HAHAHAHA! PLUS IT MEANS I CAN VALIDATE MY EXISTENCE LIKE A PARKING STAMPED TICKET HAHAHAHAHA OH LORD HAHAHAHHAHA I CAN'T STOP LAUGHING ABOUT SEX!!!! I'M LIKE ROBERT PLANT!! !I CAN'T STOP TALKING ABOUT LOVE!11 HAHAHAHAHA OH GOD SEXXXX!!1 I GOT TO REGULATE!!!! AHHAHAHA REGULATE MY TALKING ABOUT SEX!!!! OH GOD HOW CAN I BE DOING THIS IN FRONT OF MY GIRLFRIEND!!! HAHAHAHA IT GIVES ME THE EXCUSE TO WAX EMBARRASSED!!! HAHAHAH JESUS SEX!!!! AHHAHAHAHA OH LORD!!!! HAHAHAHS EX!!! AHAHHA EX!!1! SEX IS AWESOME!!11 HAHAHAH DAMN IT'S SO GOOD!!!! SEX!!!! WOW!!!! AHAHHAHA SEX!!!! WOW!!! AHHAHAHHAHAHHA EVEN THOUGH PEOPLE HAVE BEEN HAVING SEX FOR YEARS NA DYEAR AND YEARS AND HUNDREDS OF THOUSANDS OF YEARS AND THERE ARE RECORDS OF SEXUALITY ACTIVITY AS FAR BACK AS HUMAN HISTORY GOES I'LL CONTINUE TO SPEAK OF SEX AS IF IT'S SOME NOVELTY!!1 AHAHHA OH MY GOD IT'S SO NOVE1!!! HAHAHAHAH JESU CHRISTO!!! IT'S THE LATEST THING!!1! YES!!1 SEX!!! IT'S CALLED THE RADIOACTIVE FLESH!!!! IT'S THE LATEST AND THE LAST!! !HAHAHAH OH LORD SEX!!1! HAHAHAHAH!!1 GOD I CAN'T STOP TALKING AOBUT SEX!!1 HAHAHAHAHA WHERE ARE THE GIRLS THEY NEED TO /CUM/ SERVICE ME!!! HAHAHAHA LOOK!!! SEXUAL DOUBLE ENTENDRE!!!! I'M JAMES BOND!!! HAHAHAHA HE HAD A LOT OF SEX WITH A LOT OF HOT GIRLS!!! HAHAHA SEAN CONNERY HAD SEX!!! HAHAHA ROGER MOORE HAD SEX!!1 HAAAHAHAH TIMOTHY DALTON HAD SEX!!!! HAQHAHAHAA PIERCE BROSNAN HAD SEX!!!! AHHAH DENISE RICHARDS MADE OUT WITH NEVE CAMPBELL HAHAHA!11 OH JESUS CHRIST SEX!!1 HAHAHA WE'RE ALL A BIG HUMAN FAMILY AND THE TIE THAT BINDS IS THE JOKE THAT IS SEX!!1 HAHAHA OH LORD SEXXXXX AHHAHAHA I CAN'T STOP LAUGHING JAHAHAHAHA SEX!11 ORAL SEX!11 ANAL SEX!1 1GIVIGN IT UP AND LOVING IT AHAHAHAHA OH SEX SEX SESX SE SX SE S XEX EJCJJRSJF VAMPIRE BAT BITE SEX SEX SEX SEX SEX!!1 HAHAHA JESUS OH LORD!!! HAHAHA I'D GIVE UP MY WHOLE LIFE FOR SEX!!!! FOR JUST A GOOD SCREW I'D GIVE IT ALL AWAY!!! HAHAHA AND IT' BE FUNNY, TOO, BECAUSE I'D BE HAVIGN _sex_ from a lot of people AHHAHAHAHAHAHAH SEX!!! OH MAN!!! SEXXX AHHAHAHAHAHAHA ;) AHAHAHAH SEX ;) LOOK! I'M WINKING CUZ I'M TALKING ABOUT SEX!!! AHAHHAHAHA OH GOD!!!!!! SEX!!!!! YEAH MOTHERFUCKERS!!!!!!!! SEX!!!!!! ;) ;) ;) woOOOOOOOO I LOVE ME SOME SEXXXXXXXXXX SEX IS SOMETHING THAT EVERYBODY WANTS EVERYBODY LOVES AND EVERYBODY NEEDS AHAHAHHA SEEEEXXXXXXXXXX YEAH I LOVE SEX!!!!"

Kobek to Indian Outsourcing Firms — 10 July 2009

Dear Sirs,

I cannot stress how pleased I am to discover your company and the services offered — perhaps you are unaware, but many of your competitors are unwilling to provide longer pieces at cost-effective prices; as you might imagine, this puts the frugal-minded customer in a very difficult position. In any event, I am contacting you about the commission of a long-form essay.

Please allow me to provide background.

As a young adult, I was active in a digital literary environment known as 'the textfiles scene'. Recently, one of my longer works from this period has attracted significant attention from The Atrocity Exhibit, a small contemporary arts gallery located in London's East End. The Atrocity Exhibit is dedicating its upcoming Spring 2010 season to exploration of what it terms Corruptible New/B/old Medias — a catch-all for artistic expression in technologically inaccessible art forms — and, as such, they have invited me to provide a lengthy essay on *HOE #999, The Madcap Laughs*, a 20,000 word, poetic diatribe that I authored at the end of the twentieth century. This essay will be printed in a pamphlet format and available to read, and purchase, at the gallery.

Upon being approached by The Atrocity Exhibit, I attempted to write the requested essay but found myself lacking the objectivity necessary to offer appropriate comment. One of my business associates, who has had great success subcontracting literary work to firms from the Asian Subcontinent, recommended that I look into outsourcing my project.

The Atrocity Exhibit have asked for a 10,000 word essay. I am allowed freedom of format. I suggest ten sub-sections, divisible from one another. If each ran roughly 1,000 words in length, all the better. Importantly, it must be remembered that these sections must be written in the <u>first person</u>, as if by me. The illusion of my authorship must be maintained. This is the most sensitive point.

As much of the material within *HOE #999* is too dense for the uninitiated, I am attaching a rough outline of each section of the essay, along with notes for cultural icons and artistic works that are referenced, and the general thematic comments required. Obviously if you choose this assignment, I will provide denser analysis and instruction for each section. I am also attaching a sample essay, taken from some of my previous writing about *HOE* that should give a sense of the tone that I seek.

A final note: as much of the language within *HOE #999* employs a street-level patois influenced by hip hop, the poetry of François Villon, the base ignorance of youth and radical second-century Sadducee Gnostics, it can be quite obscene. Whichever staffer does the final writing will require a good sense of humour and the grace of the disinclined.

If the above and the attached materials prove agreeable, then please reply and we will move forward on this project. I look forward to a fruitful and pleasurable working relationship with you. I am,

Yours truly, Jarett Kobek

Attached Outline of Proposed Commissioned Essay:
HOE #999: Decennial Analysis and Celebratory Appreciation

Section One: On the Nature of Composition

This should discuss the method by which *HOE #999* was created—a juxtaposition of original material with digitally sampled texts found throughout the Internet, circa 2000. Most sampled documents no longer exist in their original form, making *HOE #999* the only archive of ephemeral data. Questions are to be raised about the issue of authorship—does a format which refuses to distinguish between sampled media and original text have any true author?

Section Two: Methods of Media Collision

Utilising perhaps the most scandalous section of *HOE #999*— the crude ASCII depiction of three African-American males masturbating on Jackie Kennedy at the moment of the Kennedy Assassination, accompanied by a short text caption—the dense media tapestry of *HOE #999* should be discussed. This portion of the file is a collision of Jim Garrison's *On the Trail of the Assassins*, the work of JG Ballard and the lyrics of 'Bullet' by seminal horror-punk band The Misfits: 'Arise / Jackie O, Jonathon of Kennedy / Well, arise and be shot down /The dirt's gonna be your desert /My cum be your life source /And the only way to get it /Is to suck or fuck /Or be poor and devoid /And masturbate me, masturbate me'. There is also a nod to Robert Crumb's Angelfood McSpade.

```
                a story:        the day the end will world

                It already happened. I knew it was all over when
Mogel said, "Hey, Jarett, you know, Poppy Z. Brite wrote for cDc." So I
went and looked and oh god, it was a post-mortem love letter to william s
burroughs and I just wanted to bring the whole world crashing down on my
shoulders, because clearly atlas had SHRUGGED! It was all over then all
of it all the pussy and perversion and preternatual paternity suits... It
was all over then. My grandfother sold manhattan to the white man. I am
so hot for it i am so hot for it. Please save me. Pelase please save me
from myself! I CAN"T SAVE OU! I CAN"T EVEN SAVE MYSELF! AH GOD I RETURN
TO CAILTIN'S Mp3 COLLECTION AGAIN! AHHH IN THE MIDDLE AGES THIS WOULD
HAVE BEEN WORSE THAN THE RACK!!! AHHHHHHHH

SEX IS SOMETHING EVERYBODY NEEDS I KNOW ALL THE TIME FELLAS IT'S HARD TO
USE A TROJAN JIMMY CAN'T BREATH EVERYBODY WANTS EVERYBODY LOVES EVERBODY
NEEDS FEEL ALL CLOSED IN

                HAhahah if I were the sort of fellow who cared to tell,
what stories there would be... You'd be shocked, but I can't bring myself
to do it, for a variety of reasons, but mostly because I'm too polite.
```

By expanding and explaining the cultural contexts of what appears to be an otherwise throwaway section, the method of construction reveals a dense tapestry.

Section Three: The Influence of Hip Hop

Written in 1999–2000, at the end of a decade spent completely under the thrall of hip hop, *HOE #999* exhibits—in its crudity of language and its urban concerns—a distinct influence of the final art form of the twentieth century. Self-evident.

Section Four: The Context of *HOE*

A discussion of *HOE* itself, a collection of files issued and authored across a period of years. A brief history of the textfiles medium, and *HOE*'s archaic standing as the last truly active textfile group at the end of the millennium. This will require looking through the other *HOE* files to get a sense of the other authors, of which there were hundreds. Discuss *HOE #999* within the context of a greater group effort.

Section Five: The Post-Pornographic Society

One of the most striking aspects of *HOE #999* is in its incredibly crude patois—described above as hip hop influenced—but it also borrows from the very nature of the Internet itself; a hyper-macho, hyper-idiotic youthful boasting that semi-intentionally mirrors the effects of electronic flesh transfer. What kind of language develops when you live in a society that offers copy advertising corn-battered, bitter-butter butt-holes?

Section Six: The Personal Made Unreal

Being an exploration of the idea that *HOE #999*, for all of its artifices, rhetorical and narrative devices, is an extremely personal expression of my life in 1999. If one has the right kind of map, one can travel down the byways of my interpersonal and intellectual journeys. Discuss.

Section Seven: Historical Context

Written in New York City at the tail end of Rudy Giuliani's administration, *HOE #999* is a brief glimpse of a perverse moment—the dazzling perils of pre-9/11 NYC, an awful place and time of police brutality against minorities and upper-class terraforming. The file was intended as a document of a frivolous society.

Section Eight: Zone

HOE #999 was structured around the ideal of Guillaume Apollinaire's *Zone*. Discussion of the original poem and its transcendent state and the effects thereupon on *HOE #999*.

IS THIS DESIRE OR AM I JUST LOST IN THE HEART? It's a clogged
heart full of death and despair... the egyptian children are here... They
steal a camera from an american tourist... I look at him with a mixture
of pity and loathing; I don't wish such a thing to fall on him, but then
I think it's his own fault for being so careless. I see his face and it
is a smear of hurt and pain, and I understand he is feeling, and my
loathing fades away, now I only have pity. I offer him my camera but he
rejects it. He tells me the camera was a present from his mother. I know
immediately he secretly was in love with her. Nothing I do can heal this
wound. He is as sedentary as the Chinese, the Chinois, who said to me, as
I walked along the Cliffs of Moher, "It's so beautiful." I almost died
that day. The Chinois would have been the last to see me alive. I saved
myself at the last moment. Extending my hands behind me and catching my
body as it went over the rocks. I was dead but then I was not.

    We came here for you once, when you died. But this wasn't here and
that wasn't you.

                   word up to the manthing.

    Well, golly gosh geee, Sarge, it sure has been a long time since I
done wrote something 'bout yonder TELETYPE. "Ah, so it has." Should I
drop and give you twenty? "How about you just give me some of that ol'
black magic?" You want I should write me another teletype story? "Please
do, I long for it. I long for it so. I need it like a junkie needs junk."
That bad, huh, sarge? "Yes, private, yes." Well, guess I can't deny my
C.O. anything. "NOT UNDER THE MILITARY CODE OF CONDUCT." Aren't there any
exceptions?

    "No."

                TELETYPE, REINCARNATE! Rise from your grave!

    But I can not bring back an exhausted idea. All of his life force
is gone. Let me put the carcass in the orgone accumulator and see what
will come of it. In you go, into the oven, into the accumulator, there
fatty, there... Do not cry... soon you will be ALIVE!

Section Nine: The Illusion of High and Low

Based on certain seventeenth-century alchemical principles, *HOE #999* attempts a wedding of high culture and low—this should be discussed as one of the guiding principles of my life as a writer. I have been driven from the beginning by a belief in the equal cultural validity of ephemeral waste and great achievements, and much of *HOE #999* is dedicated to the stark juxtaposition of both.

Section Ten: Youthful Failing

A contrite explanation of the methodology employed within *HOE #999* as seen through its major flaw: the excess of ambition versus the scarcity of talent and writing ability. *HOE #999* was written when I was twenty years old, and, frankly, an idiot. If this section can be as sincere sounding and contrite as possible, we'll be ahead of the game.

Sample Essay Attachment

In the days way before social networking, if you were using a modem to call a bbs, chances are that you were, in some not insignificant way, ostracised from your larger community. If you were a sixteen-year-old kid in, say, Texas, and writing textfiles, chances are that you were one of the Nerds, Freaks or Fags. There was a literal siege mentality to this kind of late-eighties, early-nineties identity politics that, with hindsight, I barely recognise. But there it was.

The files were an early form of geek-empowerment, and that siege mentality saw an adoption of a rhetorical association with genuinely dispossessed members of society—African-Americans, homosexuals, Jews and pretty much any other minority group that you could name. But this association was processed through the mentality of the same kinds of kids who would later be wearing Marilyn Manson T-shirts to BLOW THE MINDS of their classmates. It was crudely done and ultimately questionable, but not entirely unjustifiable.

The language, in particular, could be quite offensive, superbly racially explicit and unbelievably obscene: textfiles had a very punk-rock DIY aesthetic, with an inherited patois of just plain ol' street cussing, hip hop influenced slang, crude depictions of sex by people who hadn't had much of it, and god knows what else. Here I'll cop to being one of (if not the) worst offenders in the entire scene—my problem, at least towards the end—was that I was attempting what I would have considered a Whitmanesque, Kathy Acker-by-way-of-Burroughs influenced overview of American life, employing that patois, and also interjecting quotations and samplings from other sources, including, perhaps most oddly, James Joyce and GWAR. Often in the same piece.

This later period coincided, broadly, with the only time of my life during which I was almost certainly insane. I'm not sure what it was that pushed me over the edge—maybe moving to New York too young and too immature—but I can remember thoughts and decisions from this era which I now consider those of a madman. Much of this was reflected in the files, which were roughly my only outlet during that bleak, bleak time.

My approach included the frequent inclusion of my real name within the files—making me an almost unique oddity in the textfiles world, where anonymity was prized. Most authors used pseudonyms or handles—my two major ones were equally embarrassing, for different reasons. At first I was Squinky. Then I was AIDS. A legitimate issue, from a reader's point of view, is the potential of seeing my files as expressions of the first person, as genuine documents of self. Which some of the material was, but both Squinky and AIDS were in my mind as much a character as Jarett Kobek, three fictional entities that appeared within the writing.

Most of the material was plagiarised from literary sources, unspeakably obscene lyrics of the post-punk and Wu-Tang, and long defunct racist neo-Nazi Internet websites. There are one or two passages that I truly wish I had not included, or had, in some way, made more obviously not my own. These methods were, in my mind, employed as a response to what literally seemed a world coming apart; both personally and otherwise. All of the files were written while living in Rudy Giuliani's New York. A black man was shot forty-one times in the streets by the cops. There was always a sense that it would all end somehow and many of these files are attempts at reconciling that end.

I was a nineteen-year-old kid who believed himself invulnerable and impervious and the best writer who had ever lived. This ensured that the files are horrible crap, utterly embarrassing and makes me miserable to imagine them being read by others. None of them, upon a re-read, strike me as being on The Wrong Side of any issue, but rather prime examples of ambition far outpacing ability.

Allow me to state for the record: I disavow it all and apologise in advance.

- HELLO I AM MICROSOFT BOB WELCOME TO YOUR NEW HOME, THE NINTH
CIRCLE OF HELL. PLEASE CLICK ON BRUTUS GRINDING IN SATAN'S
JAWS TO KNOW YOUR PITIFUL FATE. IGNORE THE SCREAMS OF JUDAS,
SOON THEY WILL BE AS SOOTHING MUSIC TO YOUR EARS. SOOTHING
LIKE A STICK OF BUTTER IN MARIA SCHNEIDER'S ASS. SOOTHING
LIKE ON ORANGE JULIUS. EAT THE BANNANA, YOU SICK FUCKING
ANIMAL. DO YOU THINK LIFE IS EASY FOR ANYONE? DO YOU THINK
THE FACT YOU ARE MISERABLE ENTITLES YOU TO WHINE ANYMORE
THAN ANYONE ELSE? THE SECRET TO THEIR LIVES IS S-E-(x)!
MISERABLE WORLD, I CURSE THEE! I CURSE ALL OF THEE AT THE
GRANGE AND ALL OF THEE AT WUTHERING HEIGHTS WHO HAVE TAKEN
MY DEAR CATHERINE FROM ME! I CURSE HER TO HAUNT ME UNTIL MY
DEATH! I CURSE I CURSE I CURSE! AH CATHERINE WHEN WILL YOU
RETURN TO ME? SHALL I JOIN YOU IN DEATH AS A GHOST? HOW THE
CHILDREN REMIND ME OF YOU... I SEE YOU IN CATHY AND I SEE YOU
IN HARETON... PLEASE COME TO ME, DEAR CATHERINE, IT IS
MICROSOFT BOB, WHO IS AS MUCH YOU AS HE IS HIMSELF, AND I
CALL YOU FROM BEYOND THE GRAVE...

    Speaking of calling people from behind the grave, let me see how
the orgones are accumulating around the corpse of teletype. shall he be
re-animated? Shall I play herbert west?[1] I shall! I look into the
accumulator, I see the signs of life stirring, but still, teletype is not
alive... The concept has been beaten and beaten and beaten over and over
again like Stephanie Seymor... It will require more time in the orgone
accumulator... Soon, soon he will rise from his grave...

---

    1. Herbert West is the titular anti-hero of *Herbert West, Reanimator*, one of
H.P. Lovecraft's lesser efforts. As the only Rhode Island writer of any talent
and renown, Lovecraft electrified my youth. Several years after completing
IIOE #999, I moved into 10 Barnes Street, in Providence, Rhode Island. This
converted Victorian house was one of Lovecraft's residences and the address
from which he issued his most significant work.

From the Journal of the Hangman's Beautiful Daughter

i had a dream last night that i was having sex with a magickal item that was some sort of dildo made of an orange stone, maybe carnelian, and was owned by a magus, and then people, including me, were eating pomegranate seeds off my genitals, which is actually a totally disgusting thought, but, in the dream it was all very mystical and amazing and everything was bathed in light. i woke up and mailed the description of this dream to jarett, then later when i was more awake i sort of wished i hadn't.

but i have been telling him everything lately, and we're both night owls and we've been passing the nights with really long phone calls. it's been good because i'm so out of it lately that if i'm not on the phone with him, or someone, i just go stand outside and look at the moon and listen to the neighbourhood breathe and start to get really freaked out and start coming up with these weird plots and schemes. like i invent new forms of divination based on the shapes of trees. or i will call a cab and have the cabbie just like, take me for drives around town, and the conversation that comes from lonely late night cabbies and lonely late night me is never as healthy as talking to jarett about mithras or marc bolan's the warlock of love. and that is saying something.

last night we were on the phone for hours. i read his chart for him (again) and we devised a special term for having a stellium in aquarius (god he has so much shit in aquarius, even his moon and sun, which actually terrifies me since everyone i know with moon in aquarius is a cold emotional robot). we called it the SICK FUCKING ANIMAL configuration which had us laughing sooooo much. it was a good conversation, even though i started crying in the middle. what else is new. it's a little bit shameful how overwhelmed i can get by basic things.

we usually talk about his writing projects at length but last night he kept fucking going on about his hoe book. which i don't understand because for years all he talked about was his web logs and his google strategy because he was obsessed, like actually obsessed, with hiding the textfiles he wrote in the late nineties from being indexed by search engines. so he has all these pages that link to fake files that he didn't actually write? or something? i never understood what he was doing but i envisioned some sort of vast network of false writings on various machines carefully linked to one another with his name in the title of them. it's like the shimmering latticework of universal self that alex and allyson grey saw while they laid together in bed on acid, but instead, it's just a latticework of elaborate search engine deceit. all to hide some text files that no one actually cares about. i don't even care about them and i stalk everyone's everything.

Methods of Media Collision

The assassination of President John F. Kennedy is the greatest example of sticky-myth, of epochal events serving as a host bodies to parasitic stories. Giving in to the chronocentric impulse, one assumes sticky-myth as a by-product of present day media culture, but its presence has always affected civilized societies. Consider alternative narratives of Lucretia found on unearthed Etruscan vases. Consider the battle of Aten and Amun-Ra. Consider Gilgamesh. Consider al-Lāt, al-'Uzzā and Manāt. Everything is true, nothing is permitted.

Kennedy's assassination is possibly the only example of sticky-myth in which the parasites completely overwhelmed their host. You can believe that a twenty-one dollar, forty-five cent mail-order rifle is the most powerful weapon in the world, or you can believe that withered old men unable to spy effectively on mimeograph Marxists somehow orchestrated a perfect *coup d'état*.

Truth is irrelevant. The event is lost. The body of myth is the living thing. Where a person falls within its spectrum functions as a litmus test for their individual anxieties about America and its government.

In *HOE #999*, I present a conspiracy narrative of the Kennedy Assassination proceeding from the assumption that sticky-myth creates an operatic inevitability. Various elements of the crime and its attendant early conspiracy theories become necessary contextual tropes. Each new approach is best understood as individual stories determined by presentation and innovation within genre confines.

TRI ANGULATION OF FIRE:

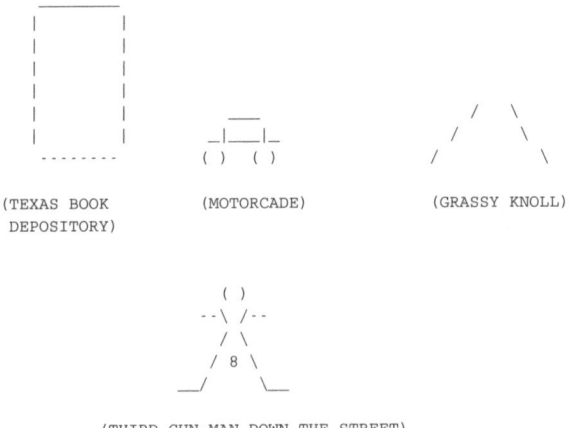

Yes, See? One man firing a load at Jackie Kennedy's warm white bitch cunt wouldn't do shit, which is why Lee "Nigger Dick" Harvery Oswald was not the lone wanker that day. Sure, he was angled perfectly to spatter his nigger cum on the Kennedys, and in particular, Jackie's sweet tasting white bitch pussy, but to ensure J. Edgar Hoover's homo-erotic fantasy of seeing three black studs with 18" dicks jerking it onto the first lady's pussy, two other men were installed. That way her white girl tang could not avoid the cum. She would get it INSIDE and on the outside, and with luck become pregnant with a spade baby; then, after she had the obvious abortion, the medical documents would be placed inside one of the FBI's famous "suicide file" and sent to JFK & Jackie in the event they ever tried to take on the FBI's authority, and specifically that of famed transvestite and homosexual, J. Edgar Hoover. The other two gunmen are not known, but are rumored to be Nigger Lips McSpade, and Strokin' Donkey Dong Jones.

The obvious major influence was Jim Garrison's *On The Trail of Assassins*, a pseudo-evidentiary encapsulation of his work as the prosecutor responsible for the only courtroom trial related to the assassination. Garrison did not invent the lexicon of Kennedy Assassination conspiracy theory, but his vainglorious pursuit almost certainly injected it on a mass scale into the American psyche. The grassy knoll, the triangulation of fire, three gunmen. Mobs. FBI. Castro. He's the man to which we owe it all.

Other influences came from the arts. In *The Atrocity Exhibition*, J.G. Ballard examines the killing through a specific lens of hypersexuality. The car becomes a machine of eros and thanos, an invasive avatar of sexual doom. Kennedy and the First Lady as bride and bridegroom riding within the prize chariot. The ultimate Kustom Kar Kommandos. 'Bullit' by The Misfits approaches the sexualised element of the Kennedy Assassination in a far cruder but viscerally more pungent attack. Written and sung by Glenn Danzig, the song presents a fantasy that links blood and healing properties with seminal fluid: 'Arise / Jackie O, Jonathon of Kennedy / Well, arise and be shot Down / The dirt's gonna be your desert / My cum will be your life source /

And the only way to get it / Is to suck or fuck / Or be poor and devoid / And masturbate me, masturbate me'.

My particular innovation was linking the assassination with the other great story of the mid-century: the social construct of the contemporary American Black. The logic of this leap seems self-evident. If we assume that conspiracy mongering around the Kennedy assassination has lost touch with reality, should we not embrace its basic unreality and give White America what it wants? From this perspective, the only way that the Kennedy assassination could have achieved any greater dramatic resonance is if the culprits were African-Americans. After all, the assassination must be the only crime in American history wherein the first impulse was to blame someone other than a person of colour.

A crude illustration is followed by what appears to be excerpts from an internal FBI memorandum laying out the conspiracy — implying that J. Edgar Hoover orchestrated the whole affair, with hints of COINTELPRO. The sexualised violence of Danzig and J.G. Ballard is carried out by racial caricatures that attack the American Princess with semen rather than bullets. The effect creates a distasteful scene of inherent repulsion. The reader is in many ways more disgusted by this fictitious version than the original violence. This beggars the question: why? Technically speaking, how is being ejaculated upon a worse fate than being shot?

The caricatures themselves owe much to Robert Crumb's blackfaced character Angelfood McSpade. The reference to one of Crumb's most controversial creations serves as recognition of the complexity in artistic depictions and discussions of race. Even for artists satirising their own race — and I point out that the satire in the Kennedy assassination section of *HOE #999* is not *about* African-Americans but the dehumanising governmental vision of mid-century so-called American Blacks—the worst is almost invariably assumed. This leaves one with several choices, all bad.

Where this section of *HOE #999* fails is in its *crudity*, in the sense of artistic ineptitude. One can sense the adolescent attempt at transgression, thrilling in its own brazenness. This undercuts the work's effectiveness. There are better approaches. As a general example, the Kennedy assassination offers a rough guide to the technique employed within the creation of *HOE #999*. Disparate strands were woven together into a tapestry towards a greater whole. Despite wearing its heavy influences, a single tone is achieved. For better or worse, the voice is mine.

In a statement, the museum said the board of trustees and its staff "are shocked and extremely saddened by this incomprehensible act that has attempted to deface an important work of art by a world renowned artist."[2]

Wooooooooo oh

    in his west german home
        in his west german home
            in his west german hoooOOooowooooome
                in his west german hooooooOwooome

2. This off hand passage gets to the heart of the matter—the backdrop of New York City in 1999, the high water mark of Rudolph Giuliani's reign of terror. A vile monster disguised as a lisping, mincing politician, Rudy personally masterminded the transformation of New York into a paranoid, money-drenched playground for the privileged and stupid.

Like any architectural project, sacrifices were made in the foundations. The victims were inevitably African or of African descent. August 1997: Abner Louima forcibly sodomized with a broomstick by four NYPD police officers in the bathroom of the 70th Precinct. February 1999: Amadou Diallo shot 41 times on the steps of his apartment by four plain-clothed NYPD officers. March 2000: Patrick Dorismond, a security guard, shot in the chest by undercover NYPD narcotics officers. Giuliani's responded by disparaging Dorismond, claming that the murdered man was 'no altar boy'. In fact, Dorismond had attended the same Catholic school as Giuliani and served as an altar boy.

Towards the end of his bloody dictatorship, Giuliani embroiled himself in art criticism. This paragraph references *The Holy Virgin Mary*, a painting by British artist Chris Ofili. Ofili's Afrocentric portrait drew the ire of Giuliani for the materials used in its construction—dried elephant dung and clipped pornographic images. The issue became a cause *célèbre* throughout the Fall of 1999, culminating in the painting's defacement on 16 December 1999. That Rudy could so easily insert himself into art criticism—demonizing the work of a black artist for negligible political gain—is a perfect summary of his racist shadow kingdom.

The best document of the period is Salman Rushdie's *Fury*—a novel focused on the banal superficiality of New York at the end of the millennium. Ignoring its many mediocrities and structural flaws, Fury gives the reader a taste of The World's Greatest City in its worst incarnation and suggests the period's inevitable violent demise. The American publication date was 11 September 2001.

Kobek to Gavin Everall — 12 July 2009

Dear Gavin,

Sorry for the delay in response — I've been at the San Diego Comic Con, delivering a paper on Romance Comics and having a minor nervous breakdown brought on by overexposure to banality.

I've gone over the contract and have no objections.

I do have what may seem like a slightly strange request. Without dictating future design, I'd ask that it be made contractually clear that the cover art in no way depict a computer, employ a black/neon green colour scheme or utilise a mono-spaced console-like typeface. This will put my mind at ease regarding what I would consider the worst-case scenario — the book's jacket looking like a Apple II/e. While the early world of computers was the home of the textfile, and the origin of *HOE #999*, much of the point is to get away from that iconography and cultural tropes of the period. Given the high quality of the designs of the books in the series, I'm sure this is an unnecessary stipulation, but it would leave me feeling at ease.

Many thanks, Jarett

```
See the three alarm fire, see the dog heat. SHE LICK HER LIPS WITH
A PASSION. in the third degree. Sometimes I cry. Yes, I cry, not a lot,
but enough to qualify me as someone who does, in fact, cry. Yes,
sometimes I weep, not a lot, but enough to qualify me as someone who
does, in fact, weep bloody tears. Salty with the blood of the undead. I
never wanna stand ya or ever reprimand ya. Dead waters rise higher than
your mind! Kreid is a feather in your cap.

WORD WORD WORD PLAY IS NOT TANTAMOUNT TO FOREPLAY BUT MY GOD IF TELLING
GIRLS YOU WANTED TO SLEEP WITH THEM SOMEHOW GOT YOU TO ACTUALLY SLEEP
WITH THEM I'D BE JOINING DON JUAN IN HELL AIN'T I JARETT "GIVE 'EM A
```

```
SPEECH FIRST" KOBEK? HELL YEAH "OH BABY, YOU KNOW, I BEEN SEEING YOU
'ROUND WE BEEN SPENDING A LOT OF TIME TOGETHER BUT UH I DON'T WANNA BE
ONE OF THEM GUYS THAT JUST SLOBBERS ALL OVER YOU I RESPECT YOU TOO MUCH
BABY SO I WAS HOPING THAT MAYBE WE COULD TAKE OUR FRIENDSHIP TO THE NEXT
LEVEL BABY AND GET DOWN" AND THEN OF COURSE, THE SIXTH MOVEMENT BRINGS
RETURN: "OH JARETT I CAN'T DO THAT WITH >YOU<!!!!! YOU'RE TOO GOOD OF A
FRIEND!!! I END UP HATING THE PEOPLE I DATE!!! I NEED TO DATE OBNOXIOUS
ARROGANT JERKS!!! I DON'T WANT TO RUIN WHAT WE HAVE WITH CHEAP SEXXX!!!"
```

Shaiz to Kobek — 13 July 2009

Hello Jarett,

Thanks for inquiring with us at outsource2india.com. We are Flatworld Solutions (owners of the website www.outsource2india.com); a global company with nine service offerings, headquartered in Bangalore, India with offices in the US, Latin America and UK.

We have been undertaking similar writing assignments globally for many of our prominent clients for years and we can definitely assist you with such projects. Basically you get writing services in India ranging from (US Currency) three cents to fifteen cents per word depending upon the type and quality required for the project.

I understand from your inquiry that you require us to write an essay of 1,000 words. You have provided detailed instructions as to what you require from us. I would like to discuss the scope of this project with my team of writers and shall get back to you soon with quotes and specifics. Meanwhile it would be ideal if you could let me know what your budget is for this particular project and how soon you would want it completed.

Looking forward to your reply. Thanks and regards, Shaiz

Kobek to Shaiz — 13 July 2009

Dear Shaiz,

Many thanks for your very quick response. I can not overstate how much it wins my appreciation.

As I mentioned in my original correspondence, I have been commissioned by The Atrocity Exhibit for the authoring of a pamphlet — what I did not mention is that this commission was for two hundred pounds sterling, which I would be willing to put towards getting the essay authored. I believe this converts out to roughly four hundred US dollars. This falls into the low end of the rates that you mentioned. In truth, I think an agreeable situation might be to have your writers put together a quicker, less researched draft than your usual standards of quality might dictate. My present concern is one of time, so if I had a text that adhered to my specifications that I could then edit later, this would be a very workable situation.

As for time constraints, I'd like to get underway as soon as possible. My deadline is not until October, so this allows for a bit of wiggle room, but I would like to get the material as soon as possible, particularly if I am going to be reworking the texts into their final version.

I hope this addition material will help guide you!

```
I accidentally left my copy of JOURNAL OF A PLAGUE YEAR in a hotel
room in san francisco. Before I even read it. I bought it at CITY LIGHTS.
I was looking for fatty fat fat Ferlinghetti. That bastard owes me $5. FIVE
FUCKING DOLLARS IS NOT A LOT OF COMPENSATION FOR THE EMOTIONAL AND ARTISTIC
DAMAGE HE'S DONE TO MY LIFE. SO HE'LL PAY, OH, HE'LL PAY OUT HIS
FUCKING NOSE.

Getting drunk all the time.
```

The Influence of Hip Hop

If nothing else, *HOE #999* is a love-letter to the musical preferences of my late teens and early twenties. Random lyrics of post-punk bands permeate invasively. One of the file's major ongoing concerns is the forever unresolved issue of Guns 'N' Roses. Even its full title, *The Madcap Laughs*, is taken from the first solo album of the late, tragic Syd Barrett.

Within this morass, a single musical influence stands out from the rest and serves as a source of pervasive thematic inspiration — Hip Hop.

Ten years later and the file appears prescient. The infection of hip hop has spread to every aspect of mainstream arts. The successful transplant of its core aesthetics obscures the fact that, as recently as the early 2000s, the music occasioned ongoing sermonising and public discomfort. Hue and cry arose over its apparent sexism, materialism, homophobia and glorification of violence. (Note: these concerns were valid. Each has been proved true a hundred of times over. And yet the Republic stands.) In the winter of 1996, I moved to Manhattan. I was seventeen years old and desperately in search of a conceptual framework through which to understand the city. I latched on to the Wu-Tang Clan, a group of nine Brooklyn and Staten Island rappers who forged their musical identities around the theology of the Nation of Gods and Earths (Five Percent), drug dealing and kung fu films. The music focused around the group's paramount desire to impose an overlapping cryptical phraseology. A metaphorical map on the five boroughs. Take the following example in which Brooklyn is represented as Medina (via the Five Percent) and Staten Island as Shaolin (after the famous Buddhist Monastery of kung fu films): 'See subway train run through the city like blood through the veins / to the heart of Medina but Shaolin is the brain'.

The city encompassed in eight beats.

(Years later, I'd come across the word psychogeography and realise that the Wu-Tang had been psychogeographers of the highest order. Operating far from academic disciplines of the white and educated classes, their work would never be viewed or discussed in its proper context. It's easier, one imagines, to moralise about homophobia.)

Vibing on the metaphysical layer of the Wu-Tang's language, I guided myself through the city. The most radical theme in hip hop was its incessant pride of place. Each and every song reaffirmed the sense that a person must never hesitate in proclaiming their origins. This transformative idea upends centuries of received notions about class and shame, achieving its radicalism through the effortless stupidity of an overtly commercialised and thugged-out voice crying, 'Brooklyn!' in the street. Growing up in Marcy Projects becomes a point of honour. You may have been born in a piece-of-shit town, but it's *your* piece-of-shit. Do not underestimate the appeal of this concept to a child of Warwick, Rhode Island.

Eventually, I realised that criticisms of rap were disguised statements of its *virtù*. Its power emerged from expression of the reprehensible, the last public forum for humour with bite. And with its emphasis on sampling and the ephemeral, hip hop was an ideal expression of a rapidly decaying postmodern conceit: the idea that *anything* could be art and any material could be incorporated. The form of the thing married to versification of bar room and barn yard humours.

While these themes emerge throughout *HOE #999*, its most visible manifestation of hip hop culture is in the repeated and consistent references to the late, lamented Ol' Dirty Bastard. Suffering from several addictions and at least one form of mental illness, his verses became stream of consciousness, slurred, half-sung. His ongoing obsession with perversity — ('Baby I'd eat the shit from right up off your ass') — proved the name was no boast. Truly, he was *old* and *dirty*.

With this utterly unique style of vocal delivery, ODB quickly became the Wu-Tang's most famous member. This fame occasioned much concern. Was his success due to talent or because his mental illness exerted a freakshow fascination on the public sphere?

At the time, I envisioned him as more than a popular entertainer. He struck me as part of a tradition of outlaw versifiers throughout the ages. Men who are not illegal but exist outside the law, creating overarching poetic systems that blanket the world. Another reincarnation of François Villon. The goal of *HOE #999* was to tap into this radical tradition of the lowly and low-down and emerge with new understanding. The third eye pried open through the indulgence of the obscene.

NEW GUNS in '00!!!!!!!! YEAH FUCK YEAH!!!!!!!! FUCK YEAH LIVE YOUR LIFE
LIKE IT WAS A COMA!!!!!   HAHAHAH!!!!! WHAT'S UP MOTHERFUCKERS?!
welcome to the guns n' fuckin roses newsletter NUMBER ONE!!! AHAHAH!!
this is the text file group about fuckin' doin what's right, ROCKIN' AND
FUCKIN' ROLLIN' UNTIL YOUR HEADS FALL THE FUCK OFF!!! AHAHAHA!!!! we have
ONLY one rule and thats: NO PUSSIES!!!!   THAT MEANS YOU JAMESY YOU
FUCKIN NIGGER-LOVER!!!!   FUCK YOU!!! YOU THINK WE GIVE A SHIT ABOUT YOUR
BULLSHIT LIES?!! EAT SHIT, FAGGOT!

    YEAH! listen this motherfuckin textfile group COMIN' ATCHA is no
fuckin' joke!! we want all you fuckin' pussies out there to know that
your time has fuckin' come!!! you hear that, JAMESY, YOU SHIT-TALKING
ASS-SUCKING PANSY!!! it's about time you fuckin' got WHAT'S COMING TO
YA!!! AAHAHAH!!! YEAH MOTHERFUCKER! just never show your face around
us real rock n' rollin' motherfuckers or i guarantee you you will get
your fuckin' ass kicked!!! we don't take excuses from nigger-lovers,
ASSHOLE![3]

    OK!! ROCK THE FUCK ON!!!!

I DON'T THINK I EVER WANNA COME BACK TO THIS WORLD AGAIN / take me away
from this modern world / I AM AXL ROSE WE ARE ALL AXL ROSE NIKE
ENDORSEMENT DAN BEN SPAZZING SWOOSH BABY SWOOOSH YEAH CAITLIN LISTENING
TO MP3S IT's THE TOURE TO END ALL TORURE I CAN'T HELP IT HELP I AM LOS IN
THIS SEA HELP HELP HELP HEP HELP HELP HEP CATS DANCE ON MY HEAD ON MY
FLOOR FUCKING GETTING BUSY ON MY COUCH

                    WHAT WAS BUGS' MISTAKE?
                        (see below)

---

3. The preceding two paragraphs are sampled directly from *HOE #379, GUNS 'N' FUCKIN ROSES*, authored by Kreid and dated 25/12/98.

In many ways, Guns 'N' Roses may be perceived as living avatars of American society at its worst: a ragtag lot of ignorant manchildren perpetually rewarded for image over content until image consumed the content. The paradox is that they were also the last great rock band. There is no greater thrill than the sleazy stupidity of their debut effort, *Appetite for Destruction*. As the group fell from (relative) grace, the aesthetic pleasure was replaced by the ongoing spectacle of Axl Rose's epic *nouveau riche* quest to remake himself as an intellectual. Truly an interest that rewards.

KPO Research Company to Kobek — 15 July 2009

Hello,

We thank you for your mail. We can undertake your writing work and execute it to your satisfaction. Our research writing rates are US$12 per page of two hundred and fifty words. For ten thousand words the total amount (including 12.5% service tax) comes to US$540.00. Payment mode is via paypal or Western Union Money Transfer or bank transfer. Payment details provided after we receive a positive reply from you.

We guarantee that there will NOT be any copying and pasting in this work. We guarantee that it will be carefully referenced.

Looking forward to providing you with this service. Awaiting your reply.

Best Regards, KPO Research Company

Kobek to KPO Research Company — 4 August 2009

Many thanks for your quick and efficacious response. As the project that I have proposed is a ten thousand word essay in ten separate parts, I would like to suggest that I commission the first one thousand word section of the essay. If I like the results, I will commission the next nine sections. I hope this will be agreeable and fits in with your schedules.

If you wish to proceed, please let me know how to send payment so that we can move things forward.

Many thanks again, Jarett Kobek

shit, well, damn, no one's really died too tragically on me,
except my aunt, but you know, that's deeply HIDDEN IN THE UNDERCURRENT OF
REALITY WHICH ONLY MY HISTRIONIC EMOTIONAL STATE CAN TAP INTO... but uh,
maybe I can pretend that I'm torn up inside over the suicide of this kid
Butthead. He was a modem guy and he knew teletype and now he's dead. He's
DEAD! It feels like a chunk of my heart is missing! A piece of my soul
evanesced into another world... How can I go on without you, Mark?
Without your butthead looking face and sounding voice? Without watching
you fuck retards on acid in the back of a cripple's van? Without her
telling me I'm a werewolf? It's a perfect day to kill yourself! God why?
I heard my sister's cry from the other room, why'd you have to pussy out?
Life could have gotten better! I would have helped you make it better but
you had to die! Oh and now it sucks for me, but I'm not going to be a
coward like you were, I'm not going to pussy out of life; I'm going to
stick it out. I'm going to brave it. I'm going to kick the world in the
ass just to show you up. You miserable bastard, why'd you have to leave
me alone? You're dead and gone and gone and dead, and I'm here by myself
wondering how I go on without you. Listen to the wind blow, I'm sad sad
without you and I miss the sounds of your 808 on the stereo. It doesn't
matter that I met you probably 4 times in my life, no, because I KNEW YOU
and you KNEW ME as soon as we met. Our minds in a perfect syncopation of
thought and being; you knew as well as I did that I would prostitute the
finer moments of my life for the sake of a joke or for a vainglorious
attempt at art, you knew all my secrets, and I knew all of yours! You
were the best friend I didn't need to speak to, because we were so close
that all of our thoughts and deeds were like the respective other's. OH
GOD, MARK "BUTT HEAD" SCHULZ, you jewish fellow, how ever am I to go on
without you? My cat's meowing it and reminds me of you. The city is
bleeding and it reminds me of you. The night is full of scents and it
reminds me of you. Everything is you and everything was you, and you are
dead and life is empty. LIFE IS EMPTY. It shall be hard for me to kick
against the pricks. I'm trapped here, but I'm not going to give you the
pleasure, hell no, I'm not going to let you see me QUIT like you did. I'm
not a coward like you, MARK "BUTT HEAD" SCHULZ, no, I'm a real person.
I'm not a hero and I'm not a brave person, but I can't do what you did.

END OF EULOGY FOR BUTT HEAD[4]

4. Eulogy for an actual person written from a fictional perspective. Mark was a friend who hanged himself from a tree limb in the City Park near my childhood home. This occurred sometime during the writing of *HOE #999*. Bearing a strong physical resemblance to the character Butt-head of *Beavis & Butt-head*, he had embraced his doppelgänger and adopted the nickname. This passage also includes an evasion typical of the period: the death of my aunt via a drunk driver was *the* defining event of my adolescence.

Two:
Well, The Best Couldn't Fucking Make It

Kobek to KPO Research Company — 17 August 2009

Dear KPO,

I have sent $54. As I mentioned in my original correspondence, I require an essay of one thousand words, related to a text of my own authorship in the past. I am including a copy of the original file.

Once I have received this first essay, if I am satisfied with the results, I would like to commission nine additional essays, each of one thousand words.

If I can in any way further assist the composition of the essay, please do let me know. Jarett

```
    I have tried to write words into a world. I may have failed. May
the gods forgive me. May the ones I love forgive me. It was enough to
create the entire world in a single microcosmic sentence, but I am a
failure, and I can not even recreate her heart, so it will take me a
longer time, a longer time, and larger amount of space to REMAKE life
into words. Why are your fingers going up my sleeve? Can you ever forgive
what I'm attempting? Will any ever see it? How many can traverse the way
down here? I don't know... YOU KNOW IF YOU DIDN'T WANT TO BE WITH ME, YOU
DIDN'T HAVE TO STAAAAAAAAAAAAYYYYYYY

    well

    it's true I can't recall San Francisco at all
    I can't even remember EL PASO, HOOOOONEEEYYYYYYY

    fair you well boys fair you well, I'm going back to Baltimore.

    I got more panchitos than a mexican; I got slick rivers like sex
lives; I stab bootlegging record executives like JAY ZEE! I slash tires
like a j.d. I break beats on the camel's hump. I SAW YOU GO BETWEEN ALL
THE PEOPLE OUT MAKING THE SCENE!

    break break your bones your heart it can all be broken with the
twist of bone or the twist of a word. Everything you were is destroyed
and pulled down like the temple in a.d. 70, everything you ever knew is
GONE. All the people you ever loved are dead, all the friends you ever
```

had are missing. What can you do? The people around you are shades from Hell, trying to drink the blood of a lamb, and when they do finally talk to you, they're hollow shells of humanity; How did you get here? How did you end up in this horrible fucking place? Where is there so much Danzig on the stereo? Could it be any worse? Could you be stuck in some texas border town looking down the sight of a gun at the greenbacks crossing over? Imagining picking them off, one by one, the women and children, their backs exploding in a fading glory of gore, and you'd be the arbitrator of life and death, for that slight moment you could be a God, but what of? Cheap trinkets and token emotions. You've given into your optimus prime evil side; now your autobot matrix is korupt and black; you actually bought into the lie everyone's always been telling you: That there is substance and there is meaning in the world. You believe it so much; there's gotta be a purpose; and then, when you look at your own life and can not help but feel the barren emptiness of the moors, you die a horrible little death inside. There's no substance here and there's no meaning here. SO YOU GIVE IN YOU SORRY SON A BITCH. YOU GIVE IN! And then your whole life became a menagerie of emotional nonsense, and you actually start to find it acceptable to sit around being miserable and depressed. You drink your depression like water from a glass. MMMMM, it's good; and then you let it motivate you and you start existing FROM IT; It becomes the center and the driving force in the lack of meaning and the removal of substance... Sucker.

A cold hard man of science brings me a glass of methadone, "Drink of this and live forever," he tells me. What can I do but oblige?

Oh yeah, let me give you some of that real life primordial realism SHIT. Let me give you some of that nicker-bocker nigger-kicking REAL LIFE In your face, gonna make you gag till you puke, bitch slipping, duck training, baby baby tregar inducing, stuff you never wanted to see, pastiche writing, Did you know I cry? I do. Not an absurd amount, but enough to substantially qualify me as someone who does, indeed, cry. That's as far as I'm going tonight. I cry. The end. Actually, my tears have overcome my intent; I'm not going to write you no primordial realism today, no sir, not I. I've given that shit up. It's bad for the soul and it's bad for other peoples' hearts. I'm not out to hurt anything anymore. Now I just want to flow like the river and Sam Cooke's jive. It's very Zen, except I don't know anything about Zen, so I can't even come close to be qualifying what is and what is not Zen. AND ISN'T THAT THE ULTIMATE STATE OF ZEN?

"Sam, he gave me orgasm," she said.[5]

---

5. In a long list of horror, this is perhaps the most terrible thing ever said by my high school friend, Sam Tregar, author of the rivetingly titled *Writing Perl Modules for CPAN*, Apress, Berkeley, CA, 2002.

The Context of HOE

In the Summer of 1994, a handful of barely literate teenagers gathered under the name of Hogs of Entropy (HOE). Their purpose: the release of sequentially numbered textfiles, providing august commentary on 'Meaningful Shit', the fatality codes to Mortal Kombat II and full collections of Nirvana lyrics. In this pursuit, the members of HOE emulated other barely literate teenagers who'd gathered under equally ridiculous names and released equally tiring files. Such collectives first emerged from the hack/phreak underground of the early eighties and quickly created a sub-literature of the profane and pointless.

The vast majority of groups disappeared. HOE was one of the few that transitioned into the age of the world wide web, a deliberately antiquated enterprise at the new frontier. Following a conscious change in editorial direction at the end of 1998, HOE began releasing files at an astonishing clip — ten files every week. (Historically, most groups released the same number roughly every three months.)

This burst of activity coincided with the development of a specific aesthetic. Until this point, the stupidity of textfiles had been a byproduct of the chance collision between sex-starved teenagers and an international distribution mechanism. Seeing the low quality of writing as a virtue rather than a deficit, HOE dedicated itself anew to the celebration of stupidity, a guiding principle that defined the output. Material was selected not on the basis of any immediately apparent literary facility, but on its ability to embody idiocy. Among the editorial staff, a general belief floated that by plunging into the moronic, and through surrender to senselessness, we achieved a new form of transcendence.

I was called back to textfiles by Mogel, HOE's new editor-in-chief. For a few issues I maintained my previous *nom de guerre* of Squinky but soon switched to AIDS, the changed name heralding a new path. I served as one of HOE's assistant editors, and my greatest triumph in this capacity was the week of all anarchy releases, with its standout file 'HOW TO FUCK UP SOME SHiT AND GET HiGH AS SHiT WiTH WiTCHCRAFT' by Killer Kreid.

I quickly became HOE's most prolific member. My early files were unthinking embraces of the stupidity aesthetic, but with time I developed a greater internal cohesion and my writing grew into poetic attempts at long monologues. I moved more towards engagement with world literature and pop culture. *HOE #999* represents the pinnacle. The earlier files were a clearing of my throat, the warming of an engine. *HOE #999* was released alongside *HOE #1000*, a true milestone. Both were enormous in scope. Unlike *HOE #999*, *HOE #1000* compiled contributions from many writers. *HOE #999* was the largest textfile ever written by an individual and almost certainly the most ambitious.

There was little response. The downside of the stupidity aesthetic was the kind of audience it attracted—a disparate group of bottom feeders with no interest beyond seeing themselves published. They offered as little as possible to get as much as they could.

Between November 1998 and December 2000, HOE distributed roughly eight hundred and fifty files. This put the group's total output at one thousand one hundred and eleven files, making HOE the most prolific of all textfile collectives. The achievement went unheralded. Other than the small cadre of writers and occasional readers, HOE shouted blindly in darkness. With its very limited raw materials and a rapidly dating technology, there was no chance of building on the group's achievements. HOE remained mired in obscurity until its final death. The last file was dated 25 December 2000.

```
All these stages of the old and the dying all these loves of the
young and the stupid all these stages of the theatrical and gay all these
lusts of the middling and ill all these copernicean dreams of my own
death at my own hands suicide you may think but i mean something more
glorious something better than mere suicide I mean to erase any existence
of my own self from this world with the power of the mind all images get
corrupted ; they're like apples exposed to the air ; i plan to corrupt my
own ; and by so distorting the image from the reality i shall cease to
exist and that manthing known as kobek will become hidden in the tapestry
backwards and never be seen again the total immolation of being

        I've grown tired at last of this ancient world... uh, I mean I've
gotten real sick of playing this orgone accumulator thing, so I'm just
gonna give you that sweet shit, that Latka Teletype shit, just give them
what they WANT! Fine, yes, fine, good. But I remain adamant; the concept
has been beaten to death; it's  dead horse; I won't write anymore files
about teletype or meenk, unless perhaps I release a uuencode of her
genitalia entitled "TELETYPE HIT THIS SHIT", but that notwithstanding, I
shall do nothing further with the theme or idea. I include it here in HOE
#999 so that the dead horse may not just be a theoretical dead horse but
may acquire the flavor and taste of putrefaction as all such things in
HOE #999 possess. yes, yes, now you know that horrid truth: HOE #999 is
to kill all and kill none. My grand endeavor, of course, will fail
miserably, but still, it's nice to see some effort come with it. some
purpose, some need; isn't it? Oh yes. Oh yes, yes, yes it is.
```

Shaiz to Kobek — 18 August 2009

Hello Jarett,

Sorry for the delay in getting back to you. A quote of US$650 is what I propose. Please let me know your thoughts and advise on how to proceed. Once we decide to go live, I will be sending you a work order draft, which you need to fill, sign and send back. I will also be raising an advance invoice of sixty-five percent of the project value. Upon receipt of your payment, work will be initiated. All the information on the deliverables expected and the inputs needed will be communicated in the work order. A writer will be designated to your project, with whom you can interact directly via skype or phone.

Please let me know when you would like to start.

Thanks, Shaiz

KPO Research Company to Kobek — 12 August 2009

Hello,

Please find herewith the completed order. The writer has said that the order is very much tougher than expected. The writer notified us that he requires more background on the history and the actual groups concerned if you require him to write the nine outstanding parts.

Best Rgds, KPO Research Company

```
Well, how was that? Did I make the grade? Ain't I a woman? AM I
REALLY REAL? Is my literary attempt 1/2 of the way towards writing
maturity? Got lucky, got lucky in time; will you beat me with a whip?
yeah yeah sexual pleasure hahahahahah SEX!!!!!! from the pain others
inflict sexual pleasure from inflicting pain; you're either one or the
other but never both. Never both. I need to see you bleed before I can
get off. It's the blood that makes life. FOR THE BLOOD IS THE LIFE. It's
a perfect day to beat your lover. the things i could tell you about her
blood red ass.

        ain't it shame to have leadbelly stab his manager on a sunday?
Ain't it a shame to beat your wife on a sunday? When you got MONDAY,
TUESDAY, WEDNESDAY, THURSDAY, FRIDAY AND Sat-ur-hamlet written by THOMAS
KYD who wrote the spanish tragedy, a play I've seen TWICE in less than a
week. Isn't that crazy? I wish I lived in England, cuz I'd just go see
the summer season of the RSC every summer. and fuck, it would rock.
```

The Ur-Hamlet was entitled _HAMLET, REVENGE!_

this is historical fact

The Ur-Jarett was called "JAROD".

This is personal fact

"But Sam," I, so called Jarett, said, "why would I want to inflict pain on her? I don't want to hurt her. I love her."

"You're a sadist, Jarett."

"I've always considered my self a secular humanist."

"A prime example of your sadism."

the ol marky-mark de sade himself was a corpulent piece of shit who didn't really practice what he preached, but thankfully popular myth and urban legend has transformed him into a startling sexual deviant, longing for the pines, giving us the hand jobs we always wanted; AAND OH HE WANTED THE PAIN but the pain was hidden in the river encased in a golden ring and the Hobbit thing fished it out, and we know what its gots in its pockets, don't we my precious?

STRIKE DOWN THE RIDERS OF ROHAN AND BURN THE BRIDGES OF MORIA FOR IT IS I, GANDALF THE WHITE, RISEN FROM THE DEAD LIKE A CHRIST ON THE THIRD DAY. LIKE CHRIST HIMSELF, I AM CHANGED; NO LONGER ARE MY ROBES GREY. I AM THE PENULTIMATE POWER. THERE IS BUT one HIGHER THAN I. THAT FLESH MAN THEY CALLED KOBEK. HIDDEN IN THE ENCYSTED LIFE OF HIS OWN SELF ONE RING TO BIND HI MATT A.K.A. STYXXXXX, I THOUGHT I'D PUT A SHOUT OUT RIGHT HERE, A SHOUT OUT ABOUT dragonlance. Fucking Raistlin Darfler, always changing her robes and going EVIL. yeah. Getting upset when I storm the closet and make her have CHAOTIC EVIL sex. It used to be NEUTRAL CHAOTIC, but now, hell, now it's CHAOTIC EVIL.

FIND THE ORBSSSS THE ORBBSSS THE ORBBSSSS

AND THE FUCKIN' LANCES

hahahha

Oberlin, the LORD OF HELMSDEEP

hahaha

or just a college in Ohio?

?!/1?!

From the Journal of The Hangman's Beautiful Daughter

i saw a furnace pink sunrise today. i woke at 6 am to get my clothes from the laundromat. i had a fantasy that neighbourhood thugs would be roaming around in my liberated madcap outfits, and would be transformed by wearing them. i can never get the smell of patchouli and incense out of stuff no matter how much i wash it, so at the very least they'd be transformed into amazing smelling hippie thugs.

i completely spaced and forgot my clothes in the dryer because everyone KEPT COMING OVER. one person would come by and then as soon as they'd left another person would knock. and everyone seemed to have some elaborate need or drama or to borrow something. it was exhausting.

after the deluge finally stopped, i talked to jarett and he seemed a little concerned and then told me he wondered if he had created the situation of my sudden popularity, because he'd written about woman, who, in addition to sharing traits with me, had a series of constant visitors and people knocking on her door. this is a person who believes that he doesn't even have to read a book to know it, though. he says he gets some kind of psychic resonance of off books, like, he can just pick a book up in the bookstore and hold it and understand what it is. information bleeds through the covers.

i didn't really have time to think or check my transits.

First we must understand that the NOSFERATU, the vampyr, in the
doorway shining so bright[6] is FOREMOST a creature of the NIGHT! He is a
killer! He is to KILL as we are to whine! It is the very essence of his
nature!

Everybody knows, everyboy knows, you only live a day, but it's
brilliant anyway.... It's brilliant anyway... ANYWAY, I'm not saying that
when I step up the mike I'm the best, just that I'm brilliant. Fuck, if
you could see my cat you'd caterwaul like Robert Plant... I can't stop
talking about love! The secrets of their lives is S-E-f(x)! I saw you
walk between all the people out making the scene... Ooooooooooh don't go
to far, stay who you are... I'm lost in that sea of sorrowful sundays,
there is a funeral procession, in the coffin is the body of Edgar Poe, he
looks at me as if it was I who killed him. Perhaps it was. I am in
Washington Square park, there is heroin in my body, I hallucinate the
ghosts of those buried beneath me and those who were hung on these trees;
the lights seem as though lit by gas. What is this world imposed over me?
I'm on a stage... atheists and christians debating... I point out
something ridiculous in the athiests' reasoning, I rush the stage, I
return to my seat, a priest turns to me and says "GOOD JOB". I am
revolted by his God. By his Christ. The only king left is King Kobek and
he is busy mentally undressing Fay Wray Darfler, peeling her clothes like
a banana... You're no good, you're no good, can't you tell that it's well
understood?

    Cntrl-G is how I get my friends' attention. Other people rely on
good characters and actually interesting personalities. I just make
computers beep. PITY ME FOR I AM THE EMBODIMENT OF THE WORD PITEOUS...
I'm an urchin lost in Oxford in 1350, the plague has hit, and it's the
little ice age. Won't you do something to save me?

    Can anyone save me???? I CAN'T SAVE YOUUUUUuu I CAN BARELY SAVE
MYSELF... Ah god, I am suffering under Caitlin's mp3 collection once
more! It's burned into my drug filled brain; forever and a day, all 22
songs will haunt me... FOREVER AND A DAY! I can not name them all. All of
them are unnameable... SWOOSH by Dan Bern... Some crap by Ani DiFranco...
some guilty pleasure by Joan Osbourne... MEN WITH HATS and their
perennial 80s hit... THEY MIGHT BE GIANTS with "BIRD HOUSE IN YOUR SOUL"
ABOUT 5 SONGS BY STABBING WESTWARD, like Chapter 12, in which it /is/

6. From 'In the Doorway', a song by The Misfits first included in the comprehensive coffin-shaped Boxed Set, a staple item of any late 1990s American music store. I attended the Boxed Set's release party, wherein every member of the Misfits—other than Glenn Danzig, the actual talent—made a midnight appearance on 27 February 1996 at Generation Records in Greenwich Village. It was here that I met Bobby Steele, former guitarist for the group. Following this meeting, I made a pastime out of reoccurring encounters with Steele. Whenever I'd spot him on the streets of the East Village, I'd cry out his name and force him into a conversation. He never, ever remembered me.

```
revealed that I CAN'T SAVE YOU I CAN'T EVEN SAVE MYSELF... Pavement's
"SPIT ON A STRANGER"... oh god, deliver me from those with crappy
taste...
```

The Post-Pornographic Society

An inherent truth of any technological development: its private use will be sexual. The history of technology is the history of fucking. Personal computers hastened a monumental leap in the availability of pornography, matched only by the so-called French prints of the nineteenth century. The origins of this leap were in textfiles, which were capable of carrying any information.

Groups like HOE eventually imposed *form* on the medium, it grew like a cancer until the medium was indistinguishable from the form. The textfile became a natural vehicle for youthful idiocy, but for many years this single colour was not the full spectrum. There was a proliferation of vastly different types of information. The medium's appeal lay in the ways it could be polluted. An open canvas. Hacking, phreaking and anarchy files each served specific roles. So too did the erotic.

There occurred a massive explosion of an entirely uncatalogued shadow literature. Well over two decades' worth of late-twentieth century pornography written by its staunchest adherents. Consumers became producers without the bottleneck of editorial control. A sample of random titles gives a sense of the exceptionally low brow and fetishist contents: 'An Incredible Affair—Electric Sex Discovery', 'Patty on a Leash', 'Roped and Raped', 'Pucker Up and Pigfuck This Pagan!' and 'Junior Sex Club'.

To give a taste of the material, here is a verbatim quote from that perennial evergreen classic, 'Let's Fuck':

'Sherry had spent much of the night reliving the event she had witnessed. The sight of her brother fucking their mom, then to see her suck his cock till it went limp, was more thrilling than anything Sherry could ever have dreamed of. She again visualised the cum spurting from the tip of John's cock and splashing across her mother's face, her eye had been hit, making her close it as she began sucking on his cock. As Sherry's mind played the night over and over again, her finger massaged her little clit, bringing her some of the thrills she imagined her mother had been having. Sherry had watched her mother and brother, now she was being watched by her sister.'

Since HOE outlasted the other textfile groups, its members witnessed the explosion of pornography across the web. In ten years, digital pornography moved from literary incarnations to static images before transforming into streamed videos. Money drove the affair: by 2000, Internet porn revenues were two billion US dollars, annually. A pornographic narrative begun within the textfile milieu intertwined with mainstream society. Taboos collapsed.

Digital pornography never lost its basic linguistic need. The text never disappeared, rather it condensed into postmodern icons of advertising copy. A new language developed, focused on the comic flexibility that dominates an adolescent view of sexuality. A place of imagination where body parts achieve impossible feats, and bodily fluids possess mystical qualities, including the ability to bestow eternal life.

As *HOE #999* attempted to mirror the surrounding society, with a particular emphasis on the digital world, its patois incorporated postmodern innovations pioneered by the porn industry. This influence is visible in the various details and repetitions around certain scatological references. The pornographic postmodern sigil only functions when repeated with enough frequency to insinuate its way into the human psyche—the inescapable disease of advertising. *HOE #999* works on the same principle, influxing repetitive structures and key phrases, obscene or not, with the intent of strophe and antistrophe. Never the epode. Filth and fury.

A familiarity with the most depraved of human acts moves through the full body of the text, giving the reader a look into the horrors of physical communication. The cloacae open wide and accept new adepts into the mystery. *HOE #999* honours and repudiates a world gone wrong, emulating the origins of a medium pioneered by the sexually dysfunctional. The worm eats its own tail. Once the pornographers abandoned textfiles, only the children were left. The stain of shame remained with us. Nothing could erase it. We embraced it.

```
THERE'S A CIVIL WAR GOING ON IN KOBEK'S BODY RIGHT WHO'S MORE RACIST
T-CELLS OR HIV VIRUS? T-CELLS CUZ T-CSELLS HATE T-CELLS TOO! THERE'S SOME
SHIT GOING ON WITH JARETT'S BODY1 THERE'S A CIVILKW AR GOING IN KOBEK'S
BODY RIGHT NOW THERE'S T-CELLS AND THE HIV VIRUS CAN'T OPEN A DISCO
WITHOUT IT CLOSING IN 3 WEEKS CAN'T GO SEE A MOVIE THE FIRST WEEK IT
OPENS WHY? HIV SHOOTING UP THE SCREEN WHAT KIND OF IGNORANT ASS SHIT IS
THIS?
```

```
         _____
        | INSIDE THIS BOX YOU WILL FIND LOVE      |
        | INSIDE THIS BOX YOUR GIRL WILL NOT      |
        | DUMP YOU INSIDE THIS BOX I LOVE AND     |
        | ACCEPT YOU INSIDE THIS BOX YOUR FLAWS   |
        | ARE ASSETS INSIDE THIS BOX NO ONE IS    |
        | BETTER THAN YOU INSIDE THIS BOX YOU     |
        | DON'T NEED TO BE A GIRL AND ALL GIRL    |
        | SELF LOATHING AND SELF HATRED DOES      |
        | NOT EXIST INSIDE THIS BOX YOU DON'T     |
        | HAVE TO ABUSE YOURSELF OR DATE PEOPLE   |
        | YOU HATE INSIDE THIS BOX IS TRUE LOVE   |
        |_____|
```

```
  But you don't live inside /this/ box. You live in the other one.
```

Kobek to Arafat Kazi — 21 August 2009

Dear Arafat,

Some time has passed since our last communication, but you'll note this is your fault and none of mine. You've exiled yourself to the dark shores of New Jersey, living in a beach house without easy access to the modern world. I hope this letter finds you in fit fettle, no worse for wear and sun-screened safely. I'm glad you've managed this little holiday and hope it treats you like a grateful servant does his generous master.

Anyway, pal o' mine, do you remember the project I've been working on? It's a retrospective book about writing from my very early twenties. Actual people from London are publishing it as a novel, which I suppose it is. Part of the set-up is that

I pitched it as one third outsourced to the subcontinent. There are poncy theoretics behind this. I contacted a few Indian KPO outsourcers and got some work off one firm, but the essay is…well, it's something. Anyhow, they're way more expensive than I had imaged. I can't justify the cost.

So here we are, bondhu, living through August in the year of Our Lord 2009, and I'm asking for your help. I must draw again from the well of infinite giving. It's time to turn to Dhaka, Bangladesh and drink deep draughts from the Black Grail. I need someone who can write my book and someone who can do it cheap. You know people, and I know you know people.

So help.

Kazi to Kobek — 22 August 2009

I have just the guy. His name is Mashruk Mohammad Nazrul and I think he has a PhD in either History or Economics from Dhaka U. (Sorry, bunky, I can't remember which!) He's the first cousin of Jon from Black, which is how I know him. Mashruk's the closest thing Dhaka has to a working writer. He did some journalism for the *Daily Star* but you'll be more interested to know that he used to write scripts for fucking *Monowar Hossain Dipjol!!!!!!* I think he did *Khaise Tore* and its sequel *Bishu's Revenge*. Given Dipjol's legal contretemps, this means Mashruk has been out of work for a long time. He's been living off inheritance since his and Jon's Dadima died. Anyhow dude, I'll mail him and make him do it. How much do you want to pay? I'll say $150 but if this is too much let me know and we can strategise a way of getting him lower.

Yr. Pal, Arafat

P.S. Since your shitty book is about the shitty writing people do when they're 21, I'm including a shitty poem from when I was 21. It's called 'Autoeroticism in the English Department'. I insist that you insert it in your shitty book. It's a sestina!

```
the day I broke up with my boyfriend,

                by little Jenn,
                        Age 13
```

My boyfriend Jim and I broke up after a few months of going out. It was very sad. He is a straight A student and I am a straight A student and we both were attracted to each other as soon as our eyes met in AP English. I have known Jim for a long time but I did not realize I liked him in that special way until our eyes met in AP English. Then I began to start feeling for him.

Our time together sure was rough. It is hard to maintain a relationship with the pressures of being smart students. Smart students take difficult courses with a lot of homework. The honors classes can take it out of you. Life is hard. Still, we managed to see each other often, and sometimes we would have parties at Jim's house for us and the other honors students. Jim's dad is the super intendant of schools and he is a good guy.

Sometimes during the parties Jim and I would go into the special closest where the action would get hot and heavy. I never took off any of my clothes and neither did he, but they were very intense experiences unlike anything I have ever felt. I did not think about sex and neither did Jim but maybe if things had gone on longer we would have had it. I am curious about sex. None of my friends have had it but I am curious about it. It seems like it could be a great thing.

Jim and I broke up last week after going for 2 months. It was very sad. I don't remember who broke up with who, but in the end, we were not together. Life is a difficult thing in many situations. I am glad I did not take off any of my clothes. I hope Jim didn't break up with me because I am ugly. I hope he didn't break up with me because I didn't take off any of my clothes. I hope he didn't break up with me to date Natalie.

The Personal Made Unreal

HOE #999 appears alien, missing the warmth of a human heart. With the expected shortcuts of the twentieth-century, storytelling became quicker and faster. It exists as itself by itself, in a world without audience or expectations of audience. No one imagined their wilful archaism would find an audience, so why bother to make concessions to them? Why not do an impersonal, impossibly weird project?

And yet a substratum of meaning transforms *HOE #999* into a deeply personal project—buried beneath the clutter are the romances, agonies, miseries, friends and family. Hidden in *HOE #999* are references to the ephemera of my childhood and adolescence. Past acquaintances make appearances, some of them unwelcome. Unrecognisable to the overwhelming majority of readers, they are nonetheless part of the tapestry.

Highbrow meets lowbrow. Porn meets stupid, another character in the narrative. Snippets appear like the masts of a ship rising above mist. True accounts, genuine episodes of feeling. Adopted materials gather around a mind exhausted by its surroundings and the weight of endured emotion. Events of happenstance related amidst fakery. The brain as an organ of torture, undergoing a perfect immolation of self. Hands of fate and circumstance. An immature adolescent from Warwick thrust into the fathomless monied depths of New York City. Trying to learn about people, wanting to learn about sex.

The life I led from the summer of 1997 until August 1998, pushed my sanity to its limits. Unbearable heat, boiling waste beneath the streets. I never went fully crazy, never became a drooling shitass, but I lost my grip on the real. I could feel the unreality of reality, like a strip of gauze layered over my eyes.

```
She loved the big lug. That's why she slept with him.

     At least that's what she claims, and in a way, I'd like to believe
it. It's a decent end to the whole fucking spectacle I have created. That
I have mocked the existence of love while trying to mock the existence of
depravity. Even if it proves to be false, and it's a way for meenk to add
yet another layer to that oh-so-well-crafted self-image, I'd like to
believe it for a little while. I'd like to believe that when the dick
went into the pussy, she really did love him. LOVED HIM LIKE HE WAS THE
GOD OF LOVE. Yeah, I see it now. the flesh parting beneath the parting
flesh, teletype's dick is the moses of her red sea of pussy flesh, and it
is not lust or the ejaculatory need that spreads the shore, but rather
love divine and incarnate in the flesh of these two miscreant misfits.

     They were in LOVE, for god's sakes! What the hell is wrong with
me? Why did I become such a vicious prosecutor of their open wound? Why
was I Pilate?! GOD I DON'T KNOW! Perhaps in a way, HOE #999 is a
testament to the size of my ego, for I have taken the entire text file
world and scene of the past ten years and not reflected upon it, nor
given it a witty, oh-so-wise theme or spin, but rather have used it as a
facet of EGO.

     You are not people, I say. I am the only person, I say. You are
mere facets of the self, I say. What self? you ask. The only true self, I
say, the self that is me, that is kObek, that is living breathing flesh
god you never tried to worship for fear he'd not answer the door.

     Suffer beneath these fists and keep your lusts trim. Keep the deep
Helm stoned and boned. Keep mogel awake and pictures of Jarett and
Caitlin atop your mini-tower. Keep the water flowering and the diet pepsi
blistering. Keep the bones rolling and the dice strolling! Keep the
balcony door shut, it's getting cold. Keep the cold open it's getting
warm. Keep the gods pacified they're getting old.. Keep the old alive
they're getting young. Keep your shoes on, they're getting muddy. keep
the mud wet it's getting bloody. Keep the blood boiling, you're getting
rheumatic.
```

You could push your fingers through it and see through the holes to the other side, but never pull it away. A gossamer web of bad craziness.

HOE #999 was not only a series of interwoven narrative conceits, it was a mirror of experienced reality. My memory of the period is hazy, incomplete. It comes back as fragments. I am in my apartment, I am not. I am in Michigan, I am in New York. I am unemployed, I am rolling in money. I am

alone, I am in love. It's the year 2000, I am in a basement
sake bar celebrating the new millennium. It's the year 1999,
my high school ex-girlfriend lives on my couch for six months.
I don't know how it looks to other people but I don't sleep
with her even once. The only coping mechanism was
HOE #999.

And in the end, writing made me well. The critical thinking
inherent in crafting *HOE #999*, the structure and order
required to make it appear unstructured and disordered
necessitated the reorganisation of my mind. Once the file
had been written and finished, I was left with nowhere to go.
I could have wallowed in bad craziness, I suppose, but it had
been exhausted. Used up. The only reward for hard work is
more hard work. Doomed to get better, wise up.

Writing can make the writer, and perhaps the reader, a better
person. To force a disordered soul into a form and coherence
of being that might otherwise be impossible. To that end,
I consider the impersonal file of *HOE #999* a success.

**Kobek to The Hangman's Beautiful Daughter —
22 August 2009**

Memo from the Hill of Dreams:

I finished reading Dan Simmons's first novel, *The Song of Kali*.
It won the World Fantasy Award for Best Novel. The WFA
is the only genre accolade that can be used as anything like
a reliable indicator of seventies/eighties quality. Example:
Robert Holdstock's *Mythago Wood* won. So did Fritz Leiber's
Our Lady of Darkness. 'Nuff said, tru believah.

Song of Kali's obvious monster is the West Bengali poet, M. Das, a leprous disciple of Rabindranath Tagore who drowns himself in the Hooghly River. His body is rescued by the Thuggee and literally resurrected by the goddess Kali, at which point M. Das starts churning out demonic verse in the service of his Lady. The narrator is an American academic (with an Indian wife!) sent by Harper's to find M. Das and bring back his new, Kalified verse for possible publication.

And when East meets West, hijinks ensue.

The book is astonishingly, almost unbelievably xenophobic. It's beyond racist. One imagines that in the year of its publication—1985, hardly a time of cultural sensitivity with Asian peoples—no one noticed. Nearly twenty-five years later, the xenophobia remains rarely mentioned. The reviews and comments I've read describe *Song of Kali* as something akin to peering over the brim of the Black Grail, an awesome look into the depths of horror. This is true, I suppose, if your idea of horror is smiling brown faces asking for rupees and making tea.

```
    James Joyce danced with Bea Arthur who hung out with Herman
Melville! Yeah!!! Call me Ismahel!!! Call me Ahab! Fucking moby dicK!
Fucking Mark Twain! Fucking Glenn Danzig! Fucking Axl Rose! Fucking yeah!
Fuckinmg hahahah!!! look I'll type my name in a random place for no
reason!!!! JARETT KOBEK!!!! hahahaha yeah!!!1 I did it!!! shit yeah!!1
JARETT KOBEK!!!!!!!!! WOOOoO JARETT KOBEK!!!!! Hahahahah my own! name!
Wow! It serves no purpose yet I can not help but type it! hahahah the
same with literary and cultural allusions! I am a pretentious art fag!
Yes! God Yes! I am attempting to prove my superiority with random
nonsense! hahahah! damn! I rock! You are all shit! Sweet Moses Ash
recording Leadbelly on the banjo of Luis Bunuel while Antonin Artaud
sucks off Anais Nin, Henry Miller not withstanding all the lust I gave to
Martis Amis and all the slutty bitches of Toni Morrison and Kenzaburo Oe
Kobo Abe Yasunara Kawabata Yukio Mishima Francis Bacon Alanis Morrisette
Tom Hanks Tom Green Tom Wolfe Virginia Woolf Ray Bradbury Isaac Asimov
Jean le Corbiellier Charles Baudelaire Arthur Rimbaud Paul Verlaine Klaus
Kinski Klaus Kinski Klaus Kinski Klaus Kinski Klaus Kinski Klaus Kinski
Klaus Kinski Klaus Kinski Klaus Kinski Nastassja Kinski Klaus Kinski
Klaus Kinski Klaus Kinski Klaus Kinsi Klaus Kinski William S. Burroughs
```

```
George Wendt Gore Vidal Dan Bern Bob Dylan Ani DiFranco beck Beck beck
beck beck KLAUS KINSKI!!!! KLAUS KINSKI!!! Beck Tom Foolery Adam Horovitz
Charles Darwin Robert Coli Sam Tregar Jarett Kobek Rita Hayworth Marlene
Deitrich Bessie Smith Missippi John Hurt Archie Bunker Jughead Spike Lee
Klaus Kinski Klaus Kinski The Artist Formerly Known as Prince Phil
Collins Robert Plant Jimmy Page John Bonham John Paul Jones Keith Moon
F.T. Marinetti Giordano Bruno Hermes Trismegistus NIJINSKI Ficcino! Pico
della Mirandola! Copernicus! Thomas Aquinas! Nicholas of Cusa! Peter
Lombard! Duns Scots! ---ABIEZER COPPE-- --THOMAS TANY-- --GERARD
WYNSTANLEY-- Andrea Dworkin King Philip Gareth Penn Sissy Spaceck Hahahah[7]
```

7. Of greatest note are Thomas Tany and Abiezer Coppe, two religious radicals of the English Interregnum.

Of the Commonwealth's many lunatics, Tany was its greatest. A Goldsmith in Temple-Bar, he suffered a stroke in 1649 and awoke with a severe case of glossolalia and the peculiar belief that he was High Priest of World Jewry. His various broadsides and tracts serve several purposes: The self-adoption of new names (most famously Theauraujohn Tany,) the laying of claim to various kingdoms, and shepherding the Jews back to Israel. Perhaps the tracts' most striking feature is Tany's unusual writing style—a dense Early Modern English routinely interrupted by his dubious Latin, Hebrew and 'Chaldean'. Among many incidents in his short career as High Priest—a time marked by habitual imprisonment and itinerant wanderings—was a day in 1655 during which Tany burned the Bible in Lambeth, crossed the Thames, and attacked Parliament with a rusty sword while clad in antique armour. (In 2003, I published a volume of all his known writing entitled *THEAURAUJOHN SPEAKS! The Collected Work of Thomas Tany*.) Coppe wrote *A Fiery Flying Roule*, the least recognised masterpiece of English literature, and was one of several figures labelled by his contemporaries as Ranters. Crafting a genuine outlaw literature based on an extreme Pauline interpretation of God's relationship with man, Coppe refutes the need for intercessors or outward ordinances. This relatively common heretical notion is taken to its logical, whoremongering extreme. The idea is best encapsulated in Chapter 2 of *A Fiery Flying Roule*: 'Well ! one hint more; there's swearing ignorantly, i'th darke, vainely, and there's swearing i'th light, gloriously'. This ethos is the distillation of *HOE #999*.

Like I said, M. Das is brought back from the dead to produce religious verse. So, yeah, he's the dead un-dead, the monster. But possibly Simmons is far more clever—'cause no matter how you read it, the protagonist/narrator is a perfect encapsulation of the clueless western tourist. The obvious monster may be M. Das, but the true monster is the ugly American, the dope blustering through his every encounter with Indians, only stopping to notice human potential when a buttonheaded bitch might be beddable. He expects servitude while protesting his egalitarianism and takes the crazy arrogant risks of someone expecting to float unscathed on whiteness alone. The narrative's power comes from the unclarity of Simmons's intent. Does the author truly believe Kolkata is a festering sore on human consciousness, or are we once more in the greedy hands of the MFA student's unreliable narrator?

What the book reminded me of, more than anything, were the French-Canadian tourists I rescued at the Ibrahim Khalil border between Turkey and Iraq. That whole trip, even before I got into the Kurdistan region, just driving around the greenish mountains of Southeastern Turkey, was consumed with the sense of being so far from home that it became impossible to remember home—either my apartment in LA or my father's pad in Izmir. I couldn't recall Rhode Island. I had entered another world that demanded the putting away of ego and its attendant misconceptions. It wasn't fear. It wasn't nerves. It was acceptance of new rules. I played the person that they wanted—the bemusing oddity of a Turkish man's quiet American son. The hardest was, as usual, faking male camaraderie. The rest was chain smoking cheap cigarettes, eating too much food, drinking too much chai and pretending to entertain people's suggestions that we get Arab whores.

```
            something old: hoe something borrowed: hoe something blue: altrocks
                         WE MAKE WAR WITH THE VIETNAMESE

     they'll korupt hoe #999 and turn it into bastion of the
bourgeoisie, yes, god knows they will. They'll take it from what it was
and they'll make it the direct opposite, not with their own generation,
of course, but with the generation that is to come. In 40 years, I'll be
helping your grand children through high school. They'll have to read me
and learn me and they'll hate me just like you hate Emily Bronte.⁸

                                  JOHN 19

     1: Then Pilate therefore took Jesus, and scourged him.
     2: And the soldiers platted a crown of thorns, and put it on his
        head, and they put on him a purple robe,
     3: And said, Hail, King of the Jews! and they smote him with their
        hands.
     4: Pilate therefore went forth again, and saith unto them, Behold,
        I bring him forth to you, that ye may know that I find no fault
        in him.
     5: Then came Jesus forth, wearing the crown of thorns, and the
        purple robe. And Pilate saith unto them, Behold the man!
```

Maybe it was 'cause I was alone, but the whole time I kept hearing Bob Dylan. 'She said / boy without a doubt / have to quit your messin', straighten' out / you could die down here / be just another accident statistic'.

The French-Canadians were flesh avatars of western assumption. The man had his MA in Mid-East Studies and thought the Classical Arabic that he learnt in Montréal would carry him through. Except he was in Northern Iraq. The Kurdistan region. Even the Arabs couldn't understand a word. Their trip hit a crescendo in Ebril, at the waterpark, where they were chased out after the woman arrived in her bathing suit. They spent a night in

---

8. And so we encounter the mystical, magickal art of writing: you can't predict how it'll happen, you won't be able to control it, and it may destroy your life in the process, but all serious writing comes true. If the reader requires evidence, the author directs them to the book held in their hands. The only surprise is that he himself is the one to korupt his own work.

a closed shopping mall and took a taxi out, that brought them to the border, where they met me. I was standing around with the safe passage drivers. And then, after they'd been bilked eight hundred dollars in twenty-four hours for taxi fares, they tried cheaping-out on the car, which was roughly forty dollars. The ride to Diyarbakir was a few hours, spent listening to the man's indignation about the Kurdish people's plight under the Turks, even comparing the PKK with the Quiet Revolution of Quebec. Small talk. The high point came when Turkish Special Forces had automatic rifles trained on the car and Monsieur Montréal couldn't stop talking about injustice. Five guns on the car and he's babbling about the unfairness of it, about how he's going to personally ensure people in the West hear about this abuse by writing an article for a Montréal newspaper. That's *The Song of Kali*. Right there.

Back to Simmons. The book hit weird—I knew it had to do with Indian people, but who'd imagine the whole thing was about Bengali writers? Fuck, there's even a scene in Tagore's house. So here I am, doing this book with Indian people and Bengalis, people hired to write for me, and I randomly end up reading a xenophobic genre obscurity about West Bengali writers. Has there ever been any other horror novel on the topic? Doubtful. And to pick it randomly. I always talk about this in vague hints, never much sense, because the topic itself is borderline superstitious. You can only approach indirectly. But it's all part of the pattern created after taking up the mystical, magical art of writing. Things begin appearing in not-so-random order, coincidences multiply, doom comes to Sarnath. You invite it in. The puzzle solves itself. It's meta-land, a funhouse reflecting infinitely into its own walls. The writing mirrors reality mirroring the writing mirroring reality. All you can do is Muslim out and submit to the unknowable, letting the narrative take you where it may.

From one perspective, none of this is particularly new — the post-sixties academic left have soiled themselves for decades with questions of WHERE FICTION ENDS and WHERE REALITY BEGINS. What is truth? What is story? Yawn. We aren't discussing conceits. Fuck theory. This isn't a parlour game between gallery openings and bong hits. This is a mode of life, a totality of existence, a way of being. A course of destiny charted. The words like fire from my fingers.

Like I said.

I don't read books. I don't write books.

I am books.

(Among other things.)

'Well ! to the pure all things are pure. God hath so cleared cursing, swearing in some, that that which goes for swearing and cursing in them, is more glorious then praying and preaching in others. And what God hath cleansed, call thou not uncleane'. — Abiezer Coppe, *A Fiery Flying Roule* (1649/50)

```
why can't you just write what you feeL? Why such labrythineeeee
ways? AYS AYS AYS DAYS HAYS KILLS YES MURDER MOST FOUL BALL NO CARLTON
FISK, IT'S A HOME RUN I SAW IT BOUNCE OFF THE POLE YES YES RED SOX WIN
GAME SIX BUT THEY LOSE GAME SEVEN; EVERY TIME SINCE 1918; SUFFER BOSTON,
sUFFRE RHODE ISLAND SUFFER FANDOM

          A brief biographical sketch of the one known as Jarett Kobek,
                  gentleman, explorer, amateur scientist,
                    deep space probe, vampire, umpire,
```

```
            statesman, 21st chromosone triplet,
             lover, beloved, burned, bored,
                  tarred and feathered

    Born in Warwick, Rhode Island on February 7th, 1978, during the
GREAT BLIZZARD. His mother required the national guard to dig her out of
her brother's house. Got to the hospital, dropped the kid. And so it came
to pass that Jarett was born and delivered in this modern world.
              and so it came to pass that you bought an illusion
                     and put it on the wall
```

Historical Context

'All the animals come out at night. Whores, skunk pussies, buggers, queens, fairies, dopers, junkies. Sick, venal. Some day a real rain will come and wash all this scum off the streets,' says Travis Bickle in *Taxi Driver*, giving voice to New York City's inchoate, one hundred and fifty year long desire. The rain fell, but no one in '76 woulda thunk it'd come in the form of a creepy little man named Rudolph Giuliani, his dark rule spanning 1994 until 2001. Rudy's mayoralty was based in three crucial elements:

1. Luck: He was in the right place at the right time, cresting on an influx of dotcom dollars and then, lingering past expiration date, his parting neatly coincided with an event that matched the wavelengths of his own paranoia and lunatic malice.

2. The self-righteous fervent hypocrisy of a former prosecutor.

3. The gumption to take credit for the successes of his first Chief of Police, William Bratton, a man so deeply influenced by Peter Ackroyd's novel *Hawksmoor* that he constructed CompStat, a statistical device of arcane crime divination. As well as monitoring citywide criminal activity, under CompStat police were directed to monitor criminal activity

on specific street corners and precinct commanders were held directly accountable for criminal activity within their neighbourhoods. With data constantly updated, the police became a proactive force, stopping trends before they became waves. Amidst this, Giuliani revealed himself to be the high priest of darkest mammon—a necromancer addicted to the oldest of the godforms, feeding on the constant churn of imaginary lucre. He personally witnessed and endorsed the terraforming of Manhattan. His goal was the replacement of the poor, of any ethnicity or race. CompStat proved the old Nazi adage: you make a place safe by putting everyone in fear. The weak were crushed underfoot and sent fleeing. African-Americans were killed by the crude tool of the NYPD, the wand of the dark mage waving over the city and affecting a transubstantiation.

Rudy was an evil cancer, his true nature was revealed years later. Bloated from fame and no longer able to hide his monstrous inner self, he slowly metamorphosed into a swollen replica of Max Schreck's Nosferatu, the vampyr, the living undead.

By the time of my arrival, New York's culture and atmosphere had suffered vicious attacks. Enough remained for me to spend several years watching the dark lord consume its energy and convert the city into his own Black Grail. One of my apartments was at the corner of 12th St and 3rd Avenue, a prostitution zone dating back decades. Now, a dorm stands on what was an empty parking lot. Its construction displaced the prostitutes into 12th Street, where they survived into the late nineties. In the spring of 1997, a series of undercover stings drove out the hookers and their johns. I watched the whole thing happen from my window. Hapless old men busted. Whores handcuffed. Regardless of the ethicality of unregulated street prostitution, this is my best personal example of New

York's transformation. Block by block by block. First the criminals, then the poor.

It was an insane place and time. Every weird element of the greater culture was inflicted upon us daily. New York became, for the moment, the capital not only of America but the world. There were brilliant parties and beautiful people, mired in the inescapable excess of post-boomer twentieth century America. *Do what thou wilt* became do whatever you want, and the slow intravenous drip, drip, drip of money and its adherents played rough on the soul. Rudy ruled over it all, his lash like fire, corrupting the city into a playground for the privileged and the stupid.

HOE #999 was constructed between October and December 1999. It was written in Detroit, Michigan, in Rhode Island and, finally, in New York City. The days ticked down to the year 2000.

```
there are dinners to be eaten in uncomfortable
silences and doors to remain shut in anger and windows to look out in
longing and pictures of yourself looking smarmy that sit on your
computer, but what the hell? WHAT THE HELL CAN YOU DO ABOUT LIFE?! IT'S
NEVER GOING TO END, NO MATTER WHAT THEY TELL YOU, AND IF IT DOES ACTUALLY
END YOU WON'T EVEN NOTICE BECAUSE IT'LL BE FINAL AND YOU'LL BE DEAD AND
THEN WHAT? THEN WHAT? . the period mistaken for a fly speck in the
penultimate chapter of Ulysses I HAVE STOLEN AND TAKEN IT TO THE FORTRESS
OF SOLITUDE


I AM HERE REPRESENTED MANY LOVE ME OTHERS DESPISE ME BUT
                UNLIKE MY FRIENDS
                    UNLIKE SO MANY POEMS
                    I AM AT THE VERY LEAST REMEMBERED
                    ONLY IN THE MEMORY OF THE FEW MAY I LIVE
                    THIS IS BETTER THAN A FATE OF ABJECT DEATH
                A FATE WHICH MANY SUFFER


        a fate which many suffer: self-loathing
```

```
              (a)  beginning of life
              (c)  adolescenceee
              (f)  early adult hood
              (h)  sometime yesterday
              (i)  middle age
              (f)  elderly
              (z)  old age
```

New York defines the file: the culmination of years living its events and suffering its miseries. The DNA of *HOE #999* is New York at the end of the millennium. The worst possible place. The worst possible time. The madcap laughs at the city, at the wild human comedy without beginning or end. You could feel it then, in the air, the blip of the self-proclaimed greatest place in the world during its last interesting phase. It thundered like a blue hammer.

```
I don't know but I gotta
do it, it's a compulsion like cockroaches covering my body, gotta do what
I gotta do so I do it and you all spew it. Spew. Dead waters rise high
than my mind. I hate all of you. Every last one of you. But you still
read on, regardless of my hate, regardless of the burning fury and
loathing that I have. Every friend I ever had is gone. Sometimes I cry.
I'm so lonely cuz I am got no homely women.

        Let's just... So you're all alone once again, and you know that
tomorrow's gonna be the same as it was today, and you can't pretend like
you're who you weren't. it'll eat you up inside like a television but you
can't say no and you can't hide and you have to do it and you don't even
seem particularly interested in the sex anymore, but still, you'll fuck
until your thighs bleed, because you're a miserable cretin, a wretch on
the face of the earth. Yeah disappointment's always there for me,
disappointment's my best friend, I hide beneath the apple tree, and all
the apples fall on me. Gonna give my heart to the pigs to roll on, and
they're gonna cool their sweatless bodies on my sorrow, yeah, it's like
water in the dirt, it makes some killer mud, oh shit, your daddy's full
of termites. Bleeding women always follow me. it was and I would prefer
not to recall it was during beauty's decline. Today in paris the women
are stained with blood.

        Sometime I'll have to edjumacate you.
```

Book Works
19 Holywell Row
London EC2A 4JB
Telephone: 020 7247 2203
Facsimile: 020 7247 2540
www.bookworks.org.uk

Book Works Publications
Contract between Jarett Kobek & Book Works
Semina 2007-2010

Book Works would like to commission you to produce a publication in collaboration with us.

Title of the book:	HOE #999: Decennial Analysis and Celebratory Appreciation
Series:	Semina No. 6
No of copies:	1,000
Launch date:	April 2009
ISBN number:	978-1-906012-21-2

Schedule for the book:

July 2009	Commission underway
15 November 2009	First draft of book to be submitted
January 2010	Editing and design underway
March 2010	Print production
April 2010	Launch date (April)

The book will form part of our Semina series.
Series Editor for this book will be Stewart Home. Assistant Editor for this book will be Gavin Everall.

Format and production details:

The Semina series will be designed to a standard identifiable series, A5 format (or smaller), maximum 48,000 words or 120 pages, no less than 30,000 words or 72 pages, soft cover, print run up to 1,500 copies.
The book will be text based, or a combination of text and image as appropriate, word count per page approx 390 per page based on A5 format.

Book Works will work with the designer Fraser Muggeridge across the series, and design and print production will be decided in collaboration with Book Works and the artist/writer.

Book Works will ensure that the cover art for this title does not depict a computer, employ a black/neon green color scheme or utilize a monospaced console-like typeface.

We would like to offer you a commission fee of £500 for all original research, and completion of the book up to production stage, materials and any expenses. Your fee will be paid in two instalments, £250 on return of signed contract, and £250 on completion of the book. Please send a receipt to Book Works for payments received.

You will also receive 100 free copies of the book, and further copies will be available to you at special discount of 50% of the retail price. No royalties are to be paid from this publication, however in the event of subsequent further editions being printed, royalties will be paid on the following basis:
1. 10% of cover price on all direct sales and trade sales in the UK and Europe, shipped from Book Works
2. 10% of net receipts on all sales through Book Works appointed worldwide distributors, including RAM in the USA, and any European or other distributor

Permission for re-printing will be agreed between Jarett Kobek and Book Works in a new contract to be drawn up in advance of reprinting.

Hey kids, it's your ol' pal AIDS here again! I know you've been
missing that voice of reason in the storm, so I figured I'd come down
from my mountain resort and give you some TRUTH. Yeah, some spiritual
sustenance in these dark times. These times where the darkies are the
darkies and the honkies are the honkies, and ain't NO MOTHERFUCKER CAN
DANCE LIKE ME.

Or like the vocalist from Cesspool, or Crepuscular, or Crapfarm,
or Candyasses, or whatever the B-Boy band that opened up on the
Danzig/SAmhain tour said, "I WANNA SEE SOME BLOOD ON THE MOTHERFUCKING
DANCE FLOOR!"

And I do. I do want to see some blood on the motherfucking dance
floor. I want it be my own blood and your blood mixing together in a pool
of BLOOD! What kind of pool did you think it would be? The buzzer ringing
at 12am kind? Nah, just pure ol' blood, sweet and sour, General Tso.

What is a conscience? well, I think a conscience is that little
voice in the back of your head that tells you what you're doing is right,
or what you're doing is wrong. Like for instance, let's say you're a
She-Wolf of the SS, the Bitch of Buchenwald. Chances are, your conscience
is telling you you're doing something wrong. But if you're some buck
toothed fat assed whiskey drink over-privileged whore from Beverley Hills
dispensing blow jobs in the Oval Office, chances are you don't have a
conscience, so the whole point is moot anyway. Yes, it's time to declare
war on L.A., and the way to do it is go down to the West Village and blow
up Monica Lewinsky's apartment. I could do it right now if I had a pipe
bomb like Eric "Columbine" Harris and Dylan "Yoplait" Klebold, but I'm
not smart enough to smuggle timers into my desk drawer. TIMERS THAT DON'T
EVEN FUCKING WORK, FOR GOD'S FUCKING SAKE! YOU CAN USE *ICE* AS A FUCKING
TIMER! I SAW IT ON MACGUYVER!

Ah, tis, tis, another crappy book by Frank McCourt, tis indeed.
Ah, begorah!, my natural Irish charm will amuse the Americans in the same
way that blackfaced Minstrel shows used to amuse them, and I'll ride it
all the way into glory ride.

well, I'm going to New Orleans, I wanna see the Mardi Gras!

got my ticket in my hand

> He calls it Arlene, after
> a favorite character in the gory Doom
> video games and books that he likes so
> much.

Dead waters rise higher than your mind...

Three:
So Here's What You Get

From the Journal of The Hangman's Beautiful Daughter

we decided to invent a new form of divination based on the shapes of trees.

i pulled ten of cups from the rider-waite tarot. i don't like the deck but it's a good card. i pull it with disturbing frequency, like if you did a statistical analysis of the seventy-two cards and how often each card is supposed to be pulled over the course of a period of time you'd find that there i had an impossible number of pulling the ten of cups. the cups rise over a joyous family, forming a celestial rainbow that radiates warmth on the farm below. typical interpretations say it signals a time of joy and abundant blessing. the scene on the card is mawkish, but there are moments in life that are of true joy, of real content. the card challenges in its demand that we acknowledge they exist, something more difficult with each year.

the ten of cups has as much depth, or lack of depth, as the person viewing. the tarot is a mirror of the universe. i don't think you can use it to tell the future but you can see where things are and where things have been. like a new way of looking at yourself, like how a pool of water reflects your face darkly and its ripples and living things alter your appearance as nature demands. it's only just a system of knowing. sometimes i wonder if books aren't like that, if books aren't another system of information that's so complex that they mirror the world.

speaking of. talked again about the hoe book. ugh. i will be glad when it's over, but he told me something i thought was totally crazy, like actually mad not just weird. he says the whole book is a rewrite of bram stoker's dracula. that its structure is the structure of dracula, a novel in letters and documents. he said in

the original of hoe #999 there's a letter from mina murray that
he made up from memory, so the idea comes from the original
file and the connection is real. the way to conceive of both
books is as interconnected works of technology haunted by
a mysterious, malicious figure. but in the case of the hoe book,
the figure isn't a vampire but rather hoe #999 itself, which
interrupts and intrudes on the other documents. he wants to
retitle the book 'the dead un-dead' after stoker's original title.

i said that's an awful title. he said it was not nearly as bad as
hoe #999: decennial appreciation and celebratory analysis.
he said it took him a few days to come up with a title that bad.

we laughed.

```
Extract from Mina Harker's Journal

     June 9th. I still have no word from my dear Jonathan. I hope that
he is fairing well in Transylvania, and will write soon. Sweet Lucy has
not yet given up her sleep walking. Only last night I had to prevent her
from perambulating to our favorite sitting spot. I looked at her face and
I saw that she was totally in sleep. The poor thing was completely
unaware of what she was doing! I locked the doors and windows to our room
and put her back in bed. I dare not tell her mother, for fear it will
worsen the woman. She already has confessed to me that her time in this
world is brief, and I would not be the one whose tongue sent her
spiraling into God's arms, blessed though they be. Nothing new to report
otherwise. I do hope Jonathan will write soon!
```

Mashruk to Kobek — 26 August 2009

After I speak again wv Arafat…I agreed to the book…he said
1 chapter…but u say 10,000 wrds…Jarret this is a lot…and u
only offer $150 AMERICAN…it means 1 taka per word…not
very much…And u say I have to write as u…so no Mashruk
bhai on the book…not so fair, brother, but I promise Arafat…

so yes, I write ur book...u say u will help me wv chapters...
I will NEED IT, brother...ur 'outline' makes no sense. What
is 'HOE'? What is 'textfile'?

My style here is different...used for quickness...don't worry
urself about that, Jarret...Mashruk will take his time wv ur
book...but will need ur help. That is all. I begin immediately.

For money...send a cheque plz...the husband of my sister
works in Gulshan HBSC...foreign fees are waived for
Mashruk.

Most very sincerely yours and in kindest regards,

Mashruk Mohammad Nazrul
Flat 8D1, Ali Huba Tower
3759 Bangabondhu Road
Dhaka, Dhaka-1000
Bangladesh

Zone

Guillaume Apollinaire (1880–1918) was the pseudonym of
Wilhelm Apollinaris de Kostrowitsky, the illegitimate son
of an Italian army officer and a young Polish noblewoman.
He was born in Rome on 26 August, 1880, and brought up in
various towns in southern France where his mother happened
to be sojourning. In 1899, Apollinaire went to Paris. Between
odd jobs as a literary hack, tutor, bank clerk, and journalist,
he managed to travel around the continent and make two
trips to London. Jovial and full of enthusiasm, he served
as the welcome companion of Montmartre's young
modernists.

He wrote fiction and poems, ultimately publishing a volume of poetry entitled *Alcools* in 1913. In correcting the proofs, Apollinaire rubbed out the punctuation and placed at the head of the collection a recent poem called *Zone*, a sort of modernist manifesto. By far the best poem of the book, it is also the most significant writing of Apollinaire's not inconsiderable career.

The narrative of the poem occurs mostly within an address of the French 'tu'. It becomes clear that the 'tu' in question is Apollinaire himself. The poem is complicated by several instances of first-person direct address, with the poet using 'je'. The 'je' of *Zone* is clearly Apollinaire himself, as the poem enforces an inherent duality and bifurcation of being, a personage whose misadventures and romantic dalliances take place against the backdrop of early-twentieth-century Paris, the other major character. The first lines bring the city into clear focus:

```
Jarod is a pretender, a very intelligent person with the ability
to slide into somebody else's personality. For that purpose, he has been
taken from his family as a child in order to work for a secret agency
called The Centre. But recently, he escaped. Jarod's new mission in life
is to help people in need with his gift, and to find out what really
happened to his allegedly dead parents.  Only, Miss Parker and her team
are out to get him...

                    OUT TO GET HIM PREGNANT

     Jarod, a boy genius with a special gift for pretending, was
kidnaped and held prisoner by a corporation that used him as a human
simulator in their clandestine research. Escaping from The Centre more
than 30 years later, Jarod now searches for clues to his true identity
and family. He also uses his ability to quickly become an expert at
anything to right wrongs and exact revenge on the wicked. All the while,
Centre operatives led by Miss Parker work relentlessly to capture Jarod,
and return him to The Centre.

                         dont ask me to keep
                         your mother chained
                         to the radiator
```

```
          she keeps bothering
          me rattling a chain
          against the metal
```

A la fin tu es las de ce monde ancien
Bergère ô tour Eiffel le troupeau des ponts bêle ce matin
Tu en as assez de vivre dans l'antiquité grecque et romaine

The Eiffel Tower cast as shepherd with its flock of bridges bleating in the morning, and, at last, tu/Apollinaire grows tired of this ancient world, is sick of Greek and Roman antiquity. These early lines are interpreted as the setting of tone, as an announcement of space between the ancient world and the demimonde. Yet *Zone* is mesmerically ambivalent. Exhibiting no fixed point in time, the poem jumps through events in the life of Apollinaire as easily as events in history, blurring into modern life all previous aviators of earlier centuries—Elijah, Enoch, Icarus, and, of course, J.C. With J.C., we encounter the true concern of *Zone*, the deep modernism of Christianity and its central resurrectionary figure, the one person capable of staying *au courant* through centuries of changing fashion.

The influence of a handful of texts dominates *HOE #999*. They are works of writers and artists in the epical form. Reflecting my tastes of the period, these texts are invoked by the form of address I adopted. Most were poetry. Some were not. The first edition of Whitman's *Leaves of Grass*, the *Jubilate Agno* of Christopher Smart, the Clayton Eshleman translation of Artaud, the work of the Ranters (specifically Abiezer Coppe), the rapping of the Ol' Dirty Bastard and Apollinaire's *Zone*. A common line runs through each. The direct address of the author in his attempt to encapsulate the world within his work; to subjugate the whole of experience within syllables. A jejune word might well be *visionary*.

The vision of *Zone* is a modernist reduction of Christianity travelling alongside the poet's meanderings through Paris, horrified by the state of the world. The women are covered in blood and beauty is in decline, religion alone remains true itself. The appeal of this vision, particularly during my years in New York, is inestimable. Unable to believe in the Christian faith, I remained willing to consider the possibility that Christ was a white magician with magickal powers giving him control over life and death. A figure like Apollonius of Tyana or Simon Magus, two of Apollinaire's aviators. This Christ, the white magician of seminal fluid, is linked with the mordant self-pity one finds in the mind of an imaginative young man on the make. I took it upon myself to render a fragmented vision of my own life. Aping Apollinaire, my text is dense with a Christianised pseudo-mysticism of the urban *flâneur* exercising middle-class privilege. The city observed without the observer becoming a part of the city. Old religion married with new religion.

```
tribute to dean the cat:
                  ecstasy in onyx

      meow. meow. meow. FOOD? meow. meow. PET ME. meow. meow. meow. PULL
THE STRING. meow. meow. PULL THE STRING. meow meow. FOOD? meow. PET ME.
meow meow meowowwwwwwooooowwwww. PET ME. TOUCH ME. FEEL ME.HEAR ME. sEE
ME. meow.

                  the world the end will day

      and behold, I did eat the book, and it was bitter in my belly.

      what auto-erotic cannibalistic sexual asphyication is this?
```

Transcript of phone call — 27 August 2009

[transcript begins three minutes into conversation]

K: Listen, you know, there's um this storyline in an old *Peanuts* collection I read when I was a kid. Not the Fantagraphics collections, but the old crappy ones from the seventies and eighties, you know, paperback sized. They're um…they used to be pretty common, I dunno, you could get them at yard-sales.

T: Right. I remember them. Yeah. We had some when I was a kid. *That's Life, Snoopy* was one.

K: God, I think everyone had some. I remember the books were narrower than the comics themselves, so they broke the strips up into weird panel formations. Anyway, there's a storyline where I think Schulz has Lucy maybe…I think it's Lucy…Yeah, probably Lucy…Anyway, Schulz gives Lucy this idea that the year she and all of her friends are living is a reused year, you know?

T: Reused?

K: Yeah, it's 1974 or whenever, but the year itself is actually recycled in some metaphysical sense from say 1953. So even though it's 1974, in some weird way, it's actually 1953. The universe cheaped-out and used an old year. People are reliving events, nothing is new. Everything is true, nothing is permitted. Some shit like that, okay?

T: OK. And?

K: And ever since I started working on this *HOE* book, it's like I've been forced to relive 1999, which is when I originally wrote the file.

T: Relive it how?

```
Let this be a warning to criminals in the future: If you're
slightly pretentious and artsy, all it takes is someone with a modicum of
writing skill and a base general knowledge of literature to bait the
trap. And then you get snared. And then you're IN JAIL, the prison of
love, but Jean Genet is neither warden NOR prisoner.

                          Love,
                             Christina

               OH DARLING, YOU KNOW YOU TOUCH ME AT THE BOTTOM OF MY
               SOUL AND YOU KNOW AS I WALK ALONG THROUGH THIS WORLD
               THAT I KNOW I'M THE DUKE, THE DUKE OF EARL
```

K: I can't explain it, exactly, it's just like shit keeps coming back. I mean, you get to be old enough, and that's all life is, right? Weird shit from the past making you uncomfortable. But this is very specific 1999 shit. The best example is like, OK, I'm in San Francisco, right? Like right now. I've been here all of August. So yesterday I'm at the corner of Sanchez and 18th, near the Castro, and I see ~~name redacted~~ walk by. She doesn't recognise me, why would she? Plus I'm dressed like the Unabomber—hoodie, sunglasses. But there she was, man, just walking on by. And I'm thinking, when was the last time I saw her? And of course it was in 1999, of course it was right at the height of when I was doing *HOE*. She came over when I was living on Thompson Street in Greenwich Village, when I was living with ~~name redacted~~, that's the last time. They were stoned rolling around on the ground together. I remember their shrill girlish laughter.

T: But what does it have to do with the book?

K: If writing is, in effect, a magickal act that binds certain thoughts and ideas to, at the least, a third-dimensional glimpse of the fourth dimension, which is both spatial and relative, and eventually everything that you write with a serious meditative intent comes true, what happens if you're dealing with an old text linked explicitly to a specific time? The whole of reality is language, codified down through the DNA, so what if the mystical, magickal act of writing reprograms the fourth dimensional totality? And then when you go back to a text, or a time, of something that already happened in a linear sense, you're inviting all of that back into your life, like with a demonic invocation. You're reusing a year. Unlike speculative writing about things that have not happened, it can't come true because it's already happened. All it can do is reappear in new and strange ways. I mean, you know, *HOE #999* itself predicts that it will be collected in a book and scrutinised by future scholars, and that's come true. You can't exactly control the accident of the predictive mechanism, like, who knew it would be me that ripped the text apart and put it into a book, but you can very well basically shape the substance. You can predict a generality but not the specific circumstance.

T: So writing is a predicative mechanism?

K: Practically. But it may be a pseudo-prophetic echo of future events. If the fourth dimension is both spatial and relative that means that time is the fourth spatial dimension, so the totality of our lives either from conception to death, or from disparate subatomic particulars that cojoin to form materials eventually fostering our conception and then go through to our death that then become disparate atomic particulars in other shapes and beings, could be viewed as a whole, like a giant slug that tapers from our mother's womb, grows larger and then tapers again straight into the grave. This theory is useful because it allows for an interpretation of various events and happenings both paranormal and deific without a recourse to the explicitly supranatural. Anyway, the point is, whenever we write a thing seriously, it might just be a third-dimensional echo of something that's part of our fourth-dimensional totality. It is a part of the totality of our being, so we can sense it in a strange way, because it is very much a part of our physical, emotional selves, but a part that we have not yet experienced with the limited third-dimensional faculties that we possess. Just because it hasn't happened yet doesn't mean it isn't always happening. So writing may not be predicative, it might just be an echo of something that we haven't yet experienced in any of our third-dimensional perceptual states.

T: But it could be predicative?

K: Also possible. It's possible that the writing itself, being made of language, which is just possibly the building blocks of all perceptual reality, functions as programming that then alters the shape and code of the fourth dimensional totality. And it might be just possible that this works better with personal prediction because there's less of a totality to shape than the whole of reality.

T: So if you were writing a book, like you are, then wouldn't it make sense to somewhere declare your own happy future?

```
Now, I like porn as much as the next guy, but shit, there isn't
anything like INTERRACIAL porn. Boy, when I seem some big black stud
just pounding his manthing away into a white bitch's pussie, boy, well, I
don't think I've ever come so hard. Those guys got dicks like TREE TRUNKS
and they're planting them in the forest CAUCASIA. Yeah, they're taking
revenge NAT TURNER style out on the bitches' cunts, they're givin' them
the what for and the whodunnit! YEAH! Ain't nothing like seeing a spade
pork a white girl.


KISS ME BAAABY GORGING HONEY'S SUNK AGAIN

        Sold into slavery down in Innsmouth, yeah, by the goddess of the
bayou light... Fucking Eliza Marsh! Fucking!!! FUCK!!!!!! FUCK DOUD!!!
FUCK!!!!!!!!!
```

K: Right, I could all be like 'Attention: Jarett Kobek will never pay to eat' and 'Attention: Jarett Kobek will achieve his every serious desire and career goal and you will love him for it.' Or maybe those are too simple, right, maybe it needs to be more specific. So in the case of the *HOE* book, which is part of this *Semina* series that harks back to this Wallace Berman pre-hippie, freak LA avant-garde, you have make a relevant prediction like, 'Attention: Jarett Kobek will betray the experimental avant-garde tradition for the sake of riches. In a year, he will be unrecognizable' and, in theory, it might come true. Possibly sooner, rather than later.

T: Good luck with that.

K: Incidentally, I also used to have this idea that if you were a writer, you'd include a passage somewhere in one of your books, a plea to future generations that would be like, OK, if you guys have time travel, just come back at the end of my life and rescue me. Wait until you know I'm on death's door, replace the body with a passable double and bring me into the future where you can heal me and show me the wonderments of tomorrow. And since time travel would obviously be the domain of the rich, I'd include a plea that was like, look, I can come and be a curiosity. The writer from the past, the most exclusive of all toys. Like Pocahontas brought before King James. I'll sing for my supper. [long pause]

Who knows, maybe it'd work?

T: I guess it would introduce a lingering question mark over your eventual death, wouldn't it?

Kazi to Mashruk Mohammad Nazrul—22 August 2009

Mashruk bhai,

Asen kemon? Bhabi baccha kemon ase? Apni ki ekhono likhalikhi kortasen naki onno kisute hat disen??? (Apni to maiyar doodh cchara jiboneo kisute hat dile amar nam Arafat na.) Ami ekhon Americaye.

The main reason ami likhtesi is that amar friend Jarett Kobek ekta boi likhtese. He wants you to write a chapter for him. Basically ore ami Dipjol-er shob video dekhaisi. O Dipjol-er khub boro fan and he knows that you're the main choreographer and lyricist.

Jai howk, oi khankir polare ami apnar address disi. He's prepared to pay up to $150 dollars. That's 10, 000 takas. Ami to bhablam je ajkal Dipjol bhai hajote poira ase, so you might be in need of some work. Goto dui bocchor dhore to no films have been made.

So, anyway, apni parle taratari amake uttor diyen. Janaiyen korben naki. I have no doubt that you'll do it. Ami oi jonno Jarettke apnar address diye dibo. He'll contact you directly.

Bhalo thaiken. Bhabike amar salam diyen, picchike amar ador ar dowa.

Arafat.

The Illusion of High and Low

A decade ago I was studying Giordano Bruno, and in particular his dialogues *Spaccio de la Bestia Trionfante* and *De la causa, principio, et Uno*. Under their sway, I developed my own interpretation based on a close textual reading. Arguing for the unity of all things, animate and inanimate, as part of the World Soul, Bruno states that anything not partaking of Truth can necessarily not exist. Nothing within this world is false. There is no untrue part of the World Soul and all are One in Truth.

My interests were not in the ontological underpinnings of Bruno's ideas but their implications. If we live in a world where all matter is part of a World Soul, and nothing untrue can exist, is it possible that all inanimate things are true? Can this be explicated to mean that we are constructed of an informational unity? If no information is false, what are the implications for 'culture'?

Our lives are yoked within enforced binary separations. In the world of aesthetic endeavour, arbitrary distinctions define the works themselves in a manner identical to the human brain's perception of colour—things are perceived in contrast with other things. Pop music is low, literature is high. Much falls in the middle. But what if no differentiation exists between human aesthetic endeavours—what if Joyce's *Ulysses* is as true, as ultimately inviolate, as 'Telephone Line' by ELO? What if apparent distinctions of quality are gauges of something else? What if high and low are defined by temporality? What if all works partake of truth equally? What if all culture just is?

Bruno was martyred twice—by the cruel justice of the Catholic Church and, much later, by the academic fantasies of Frances Yates. The latter foregrounded the influence of the *Corpus*

```
INFORMATIONAL MEMORANDUM
From: CAS Student Council
To: CAS students

The School of Education offers four courses in American Sign Language.
Heretofore, these courses could not be used in fulfillment of the
foreign-language requirement in CAS. As of this past Spring, CAS policy
has changed. The current policy is that any student who wishes to count
ASL as a foreign language can ask the Committee on Undergraduate Academic
Standards for an allowance to count it as such. (The Committee has been
instructed to grant such permission without fuss.) If you wish such
permission, fill out a petition form in the Advising Center (905 Main).

For more information on taking courses outside CAS, see an advisor in 905
Main; for more information on the ASL courses, see the Deafness
Rehabilitation Department (Education Building, twelfth floor).
```

Hermetica over Bruno to the exclusion of everything else. An examination of Bruno's work reveals this idea to be nonsense. Indeed, the only real support for Yates is the historical misunderstanding of Renaissance thinkers who established a cult based on Hermes Trismegistus, an Egyptian philosophical superhero imagined to have preceded Plato.

Like every superhero, Hermes was a semiotic wish fulfilment for the socially challenged. One text attributed to Trismegistus not found in the *Corpus* is the *Emerald Tablet*. Found in the Latin text is an idea, often reduced to, 'As Above, So Below'. This slogan, and the rest of the *Tablet*, exerted enormous influence over medieval and Renaissance alchemists. The phrase implies a unity of being through all matter, but also indicates that the alchemist's art of refining base metals exists on both spiritual and corporeal planes. The alchemist's true gold was expanded consciousness, an opening of the doors of perception to the universe's actual form rather than the low vision of corruptible flesh.

As with my interpretation of Bruno, 'As Above, So Below' can be taken as a measure of the cultural world. Taking hold was the hope that the *refiner's fire* of alchemy might be achieved through a plunge into chaos. Delirium achieved by experiencing the right works at the right time, limited to nothing. All art, all culture. The full spectrum. Cheap entertainments and acknowledged masterpieces. Anything that launches consciousness into its proper place. As above, so below.

This explains why *HOE #999*, a text relying on the history of western thought, also demonstrates a perverse interest in the musical work of Glenn Danzig. A five-foot-four punk turned cockrocker, Danzig is the embodiment of embarrassment. Particularly in 1999. But something in the music grabbed me. I attempted shamanism with the materials on hand. Some days it was Charlotte Brontë. Others it was Axl Rose. They were all the same to me—equally as meaningful, and thus, equally as meaningless.

```
Having not actually read either book, I can only proffer my
opinions on Frank McCourt and his wonderful works with the caveat that
they are based in heresay and nonsense. Well, first and foremost, you
must understand that growing up in the Irish town of Limerick was not an
easy thing for Frank McCourt.
     He suffered greatly. Of course, since I too, in my long hard
battle of a life have suffered greatly, I can not empathize nor
sympathize with his suffering. He deserved to suffer, because I have
suffered, and as I have for the most part elevated myself from my
suffering, so too do I hope that Frank McCourt did the same. What I mean
to say is, if I was exceptionally poor and then suddenly became
exceptionally rich, I would not give back any money to my urban
community. I would become as avaricious and greedy as any person had ever
become before. I would be a rap star.
     Frank McCourt's life was tough and bad. At Least I think it was,
because I haven't read either book. Somehow, my total lack of knowledge
about the books and gross ignorance about pretty much everything else in
life makes me the perfect commentator on this particular subject. And, if
you really want to know the more abstract truth, my ignorance makes me
the perfect commentator on every subject, not just that delightful Frank
McCourt.
     For instance, because I am full of shit and will never make any
sense, and never have made any sense, I am incapable of seeing how fucked
I truly am. Most decent people, upon catching a reflection of themselves
in the proverbial mirror, would cower in shame at how ridiculous they
truly are. Myself, however, am so blinded by my ignorance that I am quite
```

similar to an owl in daylight. Because I can not see anything, my
blindness empowers me to sound off on any given subject I like.
   A favorite topic of mine is this so-called "pussy stare" that men
get when they do so peruse the genitalia of women. First hand, I say, men
always seem rather befuddled upon looking down the barrel of my cootchie,
and get this dumb look on their face that reminds me of cocker spaniels
at midnight. I would propose that men get this so-called "pussy stare"
because they are enraptured with that which they can never possess. I
would propose that faced with the pussy they become dumb animals
over-awed by the ultimate unknown.
   The fact that my own genitals (as so clearly revealed in
pierce.jpg) look something like wet roast beef put through a wheat
thrasher left around to sit since last Sunday, I say again, the fact that
my own genitals look like this means nothing. Clearly when men are faced
with genitalia of the woman they become overwhelmed with the ultimate
unobtainable. It is inconceivable to me that they might just be spooked
out by my moist slathering cootchie and wonder what they have gotten
themselves into. No, this not temporal, watson, this is not elementary,
WATSON, this is a topic of universal hard-assed profundity.

                    huh huh dead people huh huh

    But the man who has made millions on his long-running sitcom, in
part, by glorifying the single life and poking fun at commitment,
eluded the press on his wedding day by using a decoy limousine.

                His honeymoon plans were kept quiet, too.

There is as much pleasure in *Tristram Shandy* as *Appetite for Destruction*. Why not force their coupling and see what offspring might be wrought from the womb?

It is not enough to reject distinctions between works of art. One must also reject art itself, all forms of self-conscious aesthetic expression. All materials are culture. Self-conscious or otherwise. Manifestations as works given the name of art. Some can tame that beast, ride it to glory. The rest provide raw material.

```
I know a girl I know a girl I knew a girl cuz know she don't wanna
know me cuz I tried to kiss her and my tongue is like a hunk of
kryptonite going up super-man's asshole, except his asshole is her mouth
and now we don't kiss no more.
     Yeah so I went on a date with this girl, and hell yeah, she was
hot, and I was like giving her my Frank Sinatra eyes, but she wasn't
having any love from ol' Drew HUNT, no, she was just giving me hate. I
tried to kiss her and she threw water on me and then and made out with a
dog named Spot. Then the dog pissed on her and threw her down a flight of
stairs and when I tried to help her up she ran to spot and forgave him.
She didn't even look at me, to see it was me who helped her up.
     Why are girls so dumb?
     Let me tell you about this other girl. well, her ass was sweet and
I loved her from the moment I saw her, so I went up to her, and I said,
"If you come with me I'll take you to Mars and I'll give you everything
you ever wanted." Then she spit on me and took up with a hooligan who
pissed on her and threw her down a flight of stairs and when I tried to
help her up she ran to the hooligan and forgave him. She didn't even look
at me, to see it was me who helped her up.
     I'm not mad, though, because I just think of some Guns N Roses
lyrics that were etched in my brain so many years ago, and this is what
I'm going to say to her, and to all the girls, and to my future wife and
soul mate someday, and she's gonna know how true it is:
```

Mashruk to Kazi — 1 September 2009

Ki obostha? Tomar ei shada friend-er jonno chapter likhte giya to dekhi boroi bipod-e porlam! What is this? 10 000 takar jonno eto khatni! Too much hard work for pennies! Ar ei shalar textfile jinish ta ki, eitai to ekhono bujhtesina!!! Amare ektu bujhaiya dao to, what is it exactly?

Ekekta chapter betare pathai, and he just complains man! Dhorjo haraiya falaitesi kintu.

Oh ha by the way, internet-e dekhlam khali Oasis vs. Blur type-er ek gada debate. I don't understand man, ei faltu duita band loiya eto kotha ken? Arey keu ki kokhono Pulp shunenai naki?!! That is the real Britpop group! Tumi ki oder 'This is Hardcore' shunso? 'Different Class' er theika much better! Ar oije *Trainspotting* soundtrack theika 'Mile End' gaan-ta,

BESHI JOSS MAN!!! Ajkal kar polapain to mone hoy eigula kisu chineo nah! Also, ajkal ami onek Manic Street Preachers shuntesi…Ager gaan gula kintu beshi joss! Kintu recent album gula eto baal-marka ken? Oi shala Richie Edwards chhara mone hoy baki member gula shob faul!

Anyway, ar ki khobor tobor amare janaiyo. Ar parle Jarret-re boilo either he pays more, or complains less.

Mashruk

Kobek to Mashruk — 4 September 2009

I've sent on the material you requested. This should be useful. It'll familiarise you with the various aesthetic and artistic predecessors—the Surrealists, Artaud, Breton, the work of Buñuel, François Villon, Céline, the glorious autobiography of Klaus Kinski—and the philosophic underpinnings. The latter skewers heavily towards Giordano Bruno, but Bruno is the big one. I've also included my footnotes to *HOE #999*, though the editors in London don't want to include them. Most will be deleted from the book. Use them as you will.

I appreciate the work you've done. Much of this can be found on the Internet, esp. the pop culture stuff, with at least terse summaries of the happenstance. If you're worried, don't be. Don't overdedicate yourself to quality. I'll go through everything before giving it to the people at The Atrocity Exhibit. Anything that needs editing or fixing or inserting, I can do. We aren't trying to have a solo performance, this is a team effort. But it goes out under my name, so I have to make sure it hits all the proper notes. We should be fine. What you've sent exceeds expectations. You've found a groove.

Mashruk to Kobek — 8 September 2009

OK Jarret…Mashruk finishes…a good job…u will like. Thx for the help…some of that was not so easy…now u have wv u all the essays…10,000 words…10,000 takas…u should be OK now with it.

U know…Mashruk wrote for Dipjol…even Dipjol was easier.

Most very sincerely yours and in kindest regards,

Mashruk Mohammad Nazrul
Flat 8D1, Ali Huba Tower
3759 Bangabondhu Road
Dhaka, Dhaka-1000
Bangladesh

```
The Symposium Lite,

                by Plato, Jr.

   Ah, greetings Xenon! I see you are on your way to the

         and that is what love is. Fuck me fickle, Alcibiates.

                    THE END
```

```
WE HAVE NO MESSAGE
SO NO MESSAGE CAN GET CORRUPTED. WE ARE SHIT SO THAT WE CAN NEVER TURN TO
SHIT. There's only one way up and over the wall. There's no obstacles for
you to climb. This is elementary my dear, this elementary, WATSON!
ELEMENTARY WATSSOOON UNDERGROUND SREET TALK SUBURBS OF NEW YORK CAITLIN
CLEANING MY APARTMENT RIGHT NOW AS I'M TYPING 22nD STREET FALLING ON YOUR
HEAD LIKE RAIN IL PLEUT I'M NOW A POEM BY VERLAINE I AM INFERIOR IN MANY
WAYS TO MY CREATOR'S LOVER'S POEMS, I CAN NEVER BE A DRUNKEN BOAT, BUT AT
LEAST I MAINTAIN A LITTLE BIT OF SYMBOLIST RESPECTABILITY IN THE STORM OF
SHIT I AM NOT SPATTERED SO MUCH AS THE OTHERS
```

Youthful Failing

If you think it's a good idea to write under the assumed sobriquet of AIDS, then you're either immature or senile. *HOE #999* is the product of a mind not fully ripened, delighting in the *grand guignol* of youth. But that's the draw of the mystical, magickal art of writing. The potential for real success admixing with the likelihood of total, abject failure. And failure comes in different forms—the least of which is embarrassing yourself. You can embarrass others, those who've done no harm. You subject yourself to inevitable and constant misinterpretation. Of course, there are no misinterpretations. All approaches are valid, but only if you like being on the receiving end of wilful malice and moron antics.

Parts of *HOE #999* amuse me with the audacity of my folly. Much makes me wince. The ugly sentences. The ill expressed ideas. The general sense of vision outpacing skill. Adolescent ideas about the grim task of writing. I mistook long labours for quick burns. I didn't revise. Everything in *HOE #999* is first draft.

Also: I was stupid. I never give full expression to my thoughts in *HOE #999*. It's half-baked, half-conceived. But in fairness, there's nothing conceptually puerile; nothing, despite the cussin' and racial epitaphs, born of ignorance. The flaws were aesthetic. My tools seem incredibly crude, relying on the semiotics of an accumulated shorthand to address complex ideas. In a word, lazy. In another, distracting. And to what end?

A story: back in the working world, I freelanced for the president of a non-profit company. A power struggle erupted on the board. Chicanery ensued. The opposition attempted to embarrass the boss through me. She sleuthed on the Internet. Somehow, she managed to confuse my race, my name, my sexual preferences and my face. But still she found *HOE #999*. I arrived one morning and found the file printed out. My boss, being a class act, summarily ignored it. I sat wondering, about writing the files, of having put my name inside an otherwise anonymous medium. And, so, I learnt regret.

The shadow of old output looms. How do you explain what you did ten years ago when there's mystery about your motivations for what you did three hours earlier? Why would anyone cobble together a 20,000 word rant at the end of the millennium? Do you tell your boss that America made you sick? That materialism and money poisoned you?

You don't. You can't.

But for the record: I apologise fully. I apologise for being young, I apologise for not knowing how to write. I should've gone into the hard sciences. But I wanted the big score, the big payment. And it comes, as sure as moons are cheeses. I feel it in my bones. But it ain't worth the headache. I coulda done it different, induced less anxiety. But then again, maybe not. The fool's journey goes past the hermit and through death until you get the world. And even then, the world isn't enough. Nothing is ever enough.

Anyway. *Mea culpa. Mea maxima culpa.*

And how exactly did you spend your early twenties?

"But, Jarett," said Caitlin, "do you really have to do this?"

"I'm afraid so," I said, and wiped a solitary tear off her cheek. In the distant sunlight her face was a plum asking to be skinned, but up close, here under the stars, it was a the lone surviving cherry blossom of a grotto long paved over and turned into a parking lot. I didn't want to cause her the pain, but there was nothing else I could do.

She said my name again, and I relished her mid-western accent. From time to time I'd teased her about it being Nova Scotian, impersonating this hacker Black Monday who used to call me up and ask about UNIX. Much laughter had by all as I made my voice a shrill blister aching out the words, "JERRETT, JERRETT, HELP ME HACK A EUNUCHZ, EH?"

I could hear, in the distance, the plaintive call of Cthulhu coming from HOE #999. He was the first text file I'd ever really taken in is a pet, and god damn, he sure was loud. Worse than my old beagle, Jasper, who had barked consistently through my entire life, and worse than my cat Dean, who talked in meows more than most people did with words.

She sighed and rolled her eyes as the calls of HOE #999 reached her. I tried to justify myself. I tried to explain that sometimes things happened in life which transcended mortal concerns, and that I could not miss a moment where my entire destiny would be decided. I was to be Lord Jim as the ship was perceived to begin sinking. Would I jump or would I stay aboard? I didn't want to make the wrong choice. This was my Lord Jim moment. But she didn't care, she didn't want to hear any of it, and I couldn't blame her.

If she had told /me/ that one of her text files, regardless of length, had become suddenly animate and required assistance in a grand journey, and that she might never come back, I'd be pretty upset. I'd be bawling, I'm sure. Out and out. So I couldn't blame her. I might have even taken it worse than she did. It was clear she wasn't going to stop me, that she would let me throw the whole thing away on what amounted to hideous pipe dream. I don't think I could have been big enough of a person to do it. It made the leaving all the more painful.

I tried to kiss her, but she wouldn't let me. HOE #999 came over the distant hills and we saw him and heard him. He cried out and I answered with a, "Here boy, here!" It wasn't long before HOE #999 was at our ankles, rubbing up against us and mewling.

"You could come with us, you know," I told her.

"No," she said, "I couldn't."

"No, no, I guess you really couldn't."

Do you know what love is? she asked me.

Sure I do.

A boy loves his text file.

Kobek to The Hangman's Beautiful Daughter—
11 September 2009

<u>Memo from the House on the Borderland:</u>

The aftermath of 9/11 brought endless babble about How Everything Had Changed. Ignoring it was the only sensible approach. For all of the horror of Dick Cheney's America, nothing shifted macrocosmically: a repressive government again waged war. The superstitious American people were afraid of outsiders. The culture was infantilised and ephemeral. Paranoia ran rampant. But at what point in our history, exactly, wasn't this true? The 1990s lured people into the false sense that Things Were Different—the great Phantom of the Eastern Bloc replaced with the excesses and pleasures of the imaginary economy. Thus the novelty of Cheney and Bush. But the stupid stayed stupid.

In the years before 9/11, Sam Tregar and I joked about the looming terrorist threat and hoped we wouldn't be in New York when the hammer came down. If a person had paid the remotest attention, they knew the inevitable future. Evidence everywhere. Before I went to sleep at 4am on 9/11, I read an article on the *New York Times* website about Bin Laden's desire to hit America. A few hours later, my girlfriend's mother was screaming into my answering machine.

The attack itself was expected. But when I went into the streets of Manhattan, I was shocked. Two cops on every corner. Ash covered cars speeding up Third Avenue. An exodus of people heading South, to walk across bridges to Brooklyn. Around 3pm, I went to the East Village and ate at the (sadly remodelled) Kiev. The radio blared news reports. Finished with my food, I made my way West.

chapter II: in which it is proved an easier
                      thing to eat cockroaches than
             carbon-14 date rats

   Having fed Caitlin's body to HOE #999, and thus severing the last
tie with this world, I decided to shed off this mortal coil.
   The glass knife was cool in my hand, and I passed it to HOE #999.
He fingered it in one paw and then passed it to the other, trying to get
ahold of its weight and shape. "Cut me free," I said. He glowered for a
moment. A silly below escaped his lips. "It's not for me to use a knife."
   his first words. I felt a father's joy as his mouth moved up and
down my body, facial hair pricking my side, as he searched for the cord
and sinew that kept soul in body. "Don't forget to free yourself
afterwards, boy,' I said. I felt an excruciating pain and heard a
crunching sound and then I felt and heard no more. I was above my body
looking down. What an ugly bastard I had turned out to be.
   I watched as dear sweet HOE #999 drew my knife to his own body and
plunged it in to that very spot where flesh became life. His eyes rolled
back and his body collapsed into a heap. I became aware of a presence
beside me, and I looked, and saw HOE #999 not as he had been in life, but
as he should have been. Beautiful and sanguine. He was a yellow and blue
striped shirt on the body of a girl. He was everything good and pure and
beauteous. HOE #999, my son, my pet, my creation. Not what I had
actually created, but what I had wanted to create. My dreams fulfilled.
Ah, love, it was good.
   "Well boy, looks like we gotta go."

Moving along Houston and Varick, navigating around police blockades. I ended up a few blocks from Ground Zero. Flames licked through the South Tower's remaining lattice work. Giant plumes of smoke came from WTC 7. A crowd of about twenty people were gathered. Half had cameras. I watched for fifteen minutes and then started back. I made it a block before WTC7 crashed. The crowd ran as if Godzilla were invading Tokyo. I ran with them. Then came the week after—a toxic miasma settled on my neighbourhood. I breathed in the dead. I got caught up in a bomb scare at Grand Central, turning the corner at 5th Ave and 42nd Street and there it was again, thousands of people screaming and running in fear.

All I could think of was Godzilla.

I don't disagree with my original assessment of *HOE #999* — a cry in the wilderness of Amreeka — but it's like an alien artifact. A relic from a distant place and time. Until today, I didn't realise why. Now I do. *HOE #999* is my final significant writing before 9/11. I've ignored it until this book forced me to the obvious.

What changed after 9/11? *Me*. Fundamentally, absolutely. You can divide my life in two, before and after, like a butcher cleaving meat. *HOE #999* is a work inviting the horror, asking it over for dinner, flirting with it. Knowing what was coming. But what happens when your invitation is accepted? In my case, perhaps predictably considering the nature of the horror, I engaged with my previously ignored ethnic origins. As I said before, my teenage years were a roundabout: would the pious son of a Muslim immigrant, an open child of the Middle East, have been any less alienated than a kid enraptured with the pseudo-nihilism of DIY and punk?

I never considered that I might be part of a continuum of Middle East identity. Despite my father being an immigrant. Despite my father being a Muslim. Because the old man was sold on America, on the flesh and culture of the Great Shaitaan. And because I was and still am sold on America. My life is off-model, not the typical experience of an immigrant child under the Red, White and Blue. Did we suffer? No. Have cultural collision? No. Experience racism, xenophobia? No.

Did the Amreeka reward me, fill my coffers with more lucre than I deserved? Absolutely.

Identity politics have membership criteria as exclusive as any country club. What the fuck were the Kobeks, other than secular Turks surrendered to sex and Hollywood? I never considered us part of the continuum because the continuum excluded our experience. From without and within, the immigrant is a figure of otherness understood only through repulsion, pity or piety.

About a year ago, I came up with the idea of *jihadpunk* and wrote a small manifesto, accepted for publication but never printed. Why *jihadpunk*? Every semi-youthful literary movement has the punk suffix appended as a masculine signifier. Good ideas need stupid names. What was the idea? Recontextualising Middle Eastern/Islamic identity through freaked out experience and avoiding, desperately, browned-out revisions of nineteenth-century melodramas. No need to ask questions answered one hundred and twenty-five years ago. YHWH, he dead. Allah too. Fuck family and fuck the old world. These raghead niggas ride dirty with Ba'al, al-Hallaj, Leila Khaled, Sean Carter and Aleister Crowley.

Then I heard of Michael Muhammad Knight's *The Taqwacores*, a samizdat novel of Muslim youth in America. And I was so happy. As the punked out child of a Muslim, and a very lazy writer, I pinned real hopes on Knight's book. I so wanted it to be good. Instead, it's the nightmare: Muslims kids dump *hijab* for the uniform of the post-post-post-punker and wallow in filth beside photos of the Kabaa, wondering aloud who they love most, Allah or Johnny Rotten. The immigrant as suffering outsider, now with shittier music. Meet the new mullah, same as the old mullah.

Allow me to suggest a different narrative. It's 29 August, 1966. The Beatles play their last concert, ever, at Candlestick Park in San Francisco. Thousands of miles away, on the same day, the Egyptian government martyrs Sayyid Qutb.

```
          HOE #999 AND I
     SAW THE PATH OF HEAVEN
     BEFORE US. WE KNEW WE
     MUST GO INTO THAT
     GREATER GLORY. IT WAS
     EVIDENT AND NECESSARY.
     THE MOON BEAMS LIT OUR
     WAY. WE WENT INTO THE
     LIGHT WHICH WAS
     PAINFUL. WE ESCHEWED
     THE LIGHT WHICH WAS
     PLEASANT. IN HEAVEN
     WE FOUND OURSELVES
     AT THE GATES. ST.
     PETER WAS THERE. HE
     HAD A BOOK. I THOUGHT
     IT WAS A BOOK OF NAMES
     OF DEEDS AND SINS.
     I WAS WRONG.
     IT WAS A PRINTED COPY
     OF HOE #999. HE ASKED
     MY FILE FOR AN
     AUTOGRAPHY. I COYLY
     TOLD HIM I HAD YET TO
     TEACH MY DARLING SON
     HOW TO WRITE. PETER
     SAID I MIGHT BE A BAD
     FATHER. I SAID IT'S A
     WICKED LIFE. HE AGREED.
     I ASKED HIM WHAT MY
     FATE WAS GONNA BE FOR
     TELLING ALL THOSE LIES.
     HE LAUGHED AND TOLD ME
     THAT MY LIES WERE SMALL
     LIES, AND THE GREATER
     SIN WAS NOT THE LYING,
     BUT THE THINKING MY
     LYING HAD BEEN ANYTHING
     IMPRESSIVE ENOUGH TO
     WARRANT A BANISHMENT
     FROM HEAVEN. I LAUGHED.
     ALWAYS THE EGOTIST.
     OPEN THE GATES, I SAID.
     SO HE DID.
```

The Beatles retreat to the studio, Qutb heads to Paradise. Pardon this truly grotesque oversimplification: in 1967, 1968, both spark a youth-based, anti-authoritarian counter-cultural movement. The cult of personality tied to a lifestyle in which repressive governmental strictures are put aside for a new Utopianism. The great boomer wave takes on an increasingly militant stance. In the West this culminates in Michael X, the Weather Underground, the Symbionese Liberation Army. In the East, it takes a little longer, but then the Shah is overthrown and the Soviets invade Afghanistan, sparking the birth of the Jihad and al-Qaeda. I suggest that these countercultures are best viewed as different components of the same machine. Sharia stands hand-in-hand with Sex and Luv and Marxism, each value set predicting the death of tyranny and extending the promise of communal self-government. On the Occident side, capitalistic culture encompasses the aesthetics of youth while discarding content. The Revolution turned into stylised advertisements for Nike. The dream dies.

Now our narrative becomes speculative fiction: what if the Sharia movement of Qutb utilised the aesthetic development of the western counterculture? What if Islamic youth were part of an artistic as well as social revolution? Imagine radical psychedelic arabesques, never crossing into idolatry, with an obvious connection to the great poster artists of San Francisco. Imagine *Jihad* magazine using Martin Sharpe's techniques from *Oz #16*. Flash forward to the late nineties and it's Riyadh and Tehran and Istanbul under attack from radical American groups. We're in Philip K. Dick territory—a place where the mechanism that eats revolution is controlled by Pan-Arabic socialists, where the tendrils of American/European idealism were never amputated. The Qutb movement is exhausted, aesthetically stripped, turned into stylised advertisements for Rotana. American radicals imperil the Islamic world.

Patty Hearst leads the SLA against the House of Saud. Hijinks ensue.

But what the fuck does any of this have to do with *HOE #999*? Simple. To get through the post-9/11 metamorphosis, you need *HOE #999*. You travel through the sordid history of growing up in Warwick, Rhode Island. I became a *sponge* for culture. I read everything, watched everything, consumed everything. This was before the Internet. When it was harder to find materials. One resorted to dubious methods.

After four years, the change was astonishing. Personally, externally. A creature of the computer transcended, gone topside. I lived in the bowels of the Internet, a Usenet flame freak clinging like bacteria to the walls of its sewers. Still learning. Learning, learning, learning. *HOE #999* was the final gasp—the last effort of the old self's construction. The monster rising up, all of its parts in place. All the rot and filth and effluvia and sick of society's base impudent desires.

Now there's this book. Its interests radically different than the file it purports to analyse. A cross-collision of culture, an injection of the Third World, an examination of money. But you can't get here without there. What is here? I'm not even sure. I won't know until it's over. It's like Harry Flashman says, 'You can always tell when something is coming to an end. You know, by the way events are shaping, that it can't last much longer, but you think there are still a few days or weeks to go, and that's the moment when it finishes with a sudden bang that you didn't expect'.

interlude: the long goodbye beholds the man

Behold the man! He is risen before you! Back and forth and over
again! He is alive and gone and dead and they stabbed Lazarus but did he
really die and I can't say! behold the man! Kobek is from the world
universal perfect makeup done by Hollywood consultants makes me the first
and the last. I am the alpha and the omega. I am the beginning and the
end. Wooooooooo little honey don't you speak money don't you bring it to
me. CAN NOT SEE YOU ANYMORE. GIRL YOU'RE SO CLOSE TO FALLING ACROSS THE FLOOR.

    I imagine you're all expecting some profound meditation which ties
it all together, which takes all the loose ends and puts them into one
ball of yarn for Dean to roll around in. You're wrong. It ain't gonna
happen little mother, so keep waiting. Filled my Diet Pepsi with
fertility drugs won't help neither. I don't need my car cleaned or
nothing stolen out of it neither. And so we have come to the end, the end
the end...

    You're a la di da driving around in flashy cars
    You're a la di da di da di da
    DI DA

    Perhaps the only final thought I can leave you with is this:
Blatant is boring. It's why I hate Ani DiFranco it's why I hate you it's
why I hate mostly everything. Anything you can say blatantly can be said
a million times better with artifice and humor. It's all too easy to
simply throw down exactly what you're thinking and feeling. It's all too
easy to make overt political statements. It's all too easy to live your
life thinking you're some hardassed motherfucker who doesn't need nobody.
Who knows all the answers and can solve all the chinese puzzle boxes. I'm
not just talking about artsy things now, I'm talking about how you choose
to live your lives.

    I don't know, maybe I'm totally wrong, but I could never live like
you do. I could never start from a point of negated reality and make the
conscious decision to stay at the point of negated reality. I could never
play the little tricks on myself, pretending like I know about the CRUEL
REALITY OF LIFE, pretending like I'm some hard assed motherfucker,
pretending that everything sucks, pretending that there's nothing out
there in the first place.

    Anyway; I think all I'm trying to say is: don't sell yourselves
short. You're probably a lot better human beings than you're willing to
let on, and it's a fucking shame to sit around pretending to be some
primordial beast who fucks, eats, shits, gets high and dies. It's a
waste.

    And you all know how I feel about waste.

Here we are, *ma chère*. And I think it's the end.

Appendix A: Excerpt of the KPO Outsourced Essay

Author's Note: *My original intent—all of the supplementary essays in this book produced by a totally anonymous information worker—hit two unsurpassable obstacles. First: the prices quoted by several Indian firms struck me as egregiously expensive. Second: the quality was disastrous. Included below is an excerpt of an essay for which I paid $54(US).*

The so-called new generation, I prefer the word kids, will find the discussion equivalent to a reading an autobiography of a dinosaur. If kids read at all that is. The millennium is just nine years behind, but nine years have brought forth changes that for the last thousand years were believed to be impossible. So be it with the textfiles. Like Microsoft once declared 'DOS is dead,' must we declare that textfiles and text is dead? What text? and why text? When you can literally expose yourself and speak, dance and do things including screwing your girl online for all to see, and all for free, When you have videos, can chat live, why Text? The text is now reserved for the SMS messages on cell phones which have a unique jargon and changed the language for ever. HRU being the short for how are you have their origins from the chat rooms where text was used with niggardliness. OK we can say that HOE is a part of the history of textfiles. So what is s great about these files that appear to be a primitive form of journals posted by electronically challenged Dodos of yesteryears?

HOE #999 thus is a relic from the past. Like all relics of the past it has an aura of struggle, freedom, and a mystique that ought to be preserved and kept for the future, when the Kids of today become mature and want to tell their kids how advanced they were from the ancients a millennium ago. In truth the textfiles of the millennium are the apex of a freedom struggle that was going on with the generations of the nineteen-nineties. There was a way to break the pressure of the stuff that welled inside the cranium and find a willing listener. One could not go to the bar and spill out the stuff there. There were social taboos and some do exist today too. The bar had limitations. One had to think and then record what one thought in some medium and then corner the listener. The problem was that the listener could as well take it to be a drunk's babble.

Sometimes Uncle Sam (Or any Local GESTAPO) may not take kindly to the profound thought that issued from the cranium. There was a mounting pressure to release on an unsuspecting world at large, the great mental anguish, and the close of the millennium provided to the select kids in the last era of the century, a medium to download their mental excreta anonymously and with fancy names on other fellow creatures who were hooked to the wires and modems of the deliverer. These people addicted to and the slave of a rectangular gadget with a black monitor on top were called 'nerds' and they were guilty of not only creating electronic magazines, but also creating songs, lyrics, music and stuff that otherwise would have required a lot of investment in things like musicians, poets, printing press and so forth.

It was no doubt the first step to a new-found freedom, a white wall on which you could type with mistakes and all, ANTHING you wanted and send it to willing fellow participants. The replies and postings grew phenomenally. There were many exchanges of textfiles, some related to politics, some to private exchanges, but we have to be charitable to the many or majority who uploaded in words, the sexual desires, and anything and everything. That was the original freedom that these spectacled and buck-toothed guys wanted as freedom, and thankfully the year 1984 which gave us the networking and Internet went on without George Orwell's Big Brother materialising on the net to curb the mental roses and metal songs, mental screws, and shit that were all parcelled into ASCII and left about to stink up minds (or so it was objected to) But it was an opening that the sidelined could use with gusto. Thus there was The simple Clerk, Sales man, the anarchist, communist, Racists, Rapists, homosexuals, whores, pornographers, lesbians, and of course the geek, and on the other side the ordinary men tempted to enter the world of new-found freedom to do or be as one pleased, and to exhibit with poorly scanned pictures and added text what one normally did in the closet.

The anguish and pain which comes from within is not for any one community though Hoe has a lot of Black writings some of them very mature and sensible, while others appear to be childish compared to the gross vulgarity and no hold barred display of the modern media. Yes there were contributors who did perk up the general content; there were those who showed us that it would not be pleasant for the little Red Riding Hoods to encounter them in deserted alleys. As it is today, in this stream then too anonymity was a sacred thing. It was freedom. May be it was not the same type that freedom signifies in history as in 1776 for example. But it was an expression of freedom that the PC and the Internet gave to the surfer who lived, dated, and even had the commode fixed under the chair so that he or she need not get up from before the monitor. Thus you have to give in to the fact that it was a representation of a culture that then merged as technology grew into things we have now. *HOE E'ZINE #999* may be now history, but it IS HISTORY…

Appendix B: 'Auto-Eroticism in the English Department (2003)' by Arafat Kazi

Author's Note: *Against the wishes and better judgement of his editors, the author pays a debt and presents 'Auto-Eroticism in the English Department,' a poem written by Arafat Kazi, age twenty-one. (For the record: no one can be from an estuary. That dude was raised in a delta.)*

Cheap beer met hollow draughts of doom, estuary
of piss and sweat that I licked from the seat
of the English Department toilet. I thought: poetically,
politically, maybe something would link to my act
of selflessly onanistic mumbo solo jumbo
flagellation that would be interpreted erotically.

Pop-eyed, I scratched my balls. Unwedged erotically
my boxers; fundamentally untrained, jumbo
in size, lowly lowing from the seat
in helpless flatulence, wishing poetically
that this endlessly symbolic estuary
of my tongue and her urine was a symbolic act.

Facts intact, tacked unto my act,
loving the self in my selfless Boeing Jumbo
flights of proto-Islamic estuary,
(Migration meets Homelessness, Motherland), poetically
where salt and water mix, tasting erotically
like stale Lite beer (but from her pulsating seat).

Like a pale, dewy raindrop on a rosebud (a seat
on a toilet in the English Department), poetically
juxtaposed like a zedonk of my soul and my act,
there was a meeting of cultures: Mumbo Jumbo

of the East meets plumbing and disdain, erotically,
hopelessly, of the Western Hemisphere. (An estuary?)

It should be noted here that I am from an estuary.
The Brits and the Bangla, mixed in riotous act,
with some American consumption
   (no consummation, not poetically)
thrown in. I am cross-linked, not erotically
(rather sad, that) but in cross-culture: the seat
of my history and where-I-come-from is a mixture
   mighty jumbo.

And so I lick pee from peehole, jumbo
fat man pervert. It doesn't do erotically,
or turns you off, but please respect my act.
Even if I'm not an epassionating estuary
of many lands and stories, seat
yourself in empathy while I minstrel on poetically.

The new estuary is of my seed and my act.
Failed and miseried erotically, I resume my seat,
jumboing beside her, and read from Milton poetically.

Appendix C: Three Editorial Communiqués

Author's Note: *The editorial process that created the text you now hold in your hands was far too protracted to represent in its entirety. The three communiqués below (which have been edited and shortened) will, however, give some idea of how this book came together from first draft to publication.*

From: Stewart Home to Jarett Kobek, 4 October 2009

Hi Jarett,

The basic structure of the first draft of *HOE #999* is solid, so there are no major revisions needed in terms of ordering the ms. But I do want to clean up the prose and also cut to tighten things up.

My main concern is that the poor sentence construction of the critical sections drags the entire book down. I think we'd gain a lot and lose very little by you re-writing these passages into good English. Doing this will also compress the information within them, and I would envisage this reducing their length by as much as 50 per cent which I don't think is a problem because they are flabby as they currently stand (I realise intentionally as far as you are concerned). Since you make it clear in terms of the narrative that you might re-edit the material you've 'farmed out to essay mills', I don't feel poor English is required to signify their origin. I haven't touched this. I want you to sort it out.

I've done a light edit on the letters between you and various other parties; see the attached version of the ms.

Most of the documents that provide 'proof' of the use of the essay mill I'd rather lose, perhaps your point is that they could be easily faked—but I think the text without these gives the reader enough to mull over. So the transaction details on page 48 and the reproduced cheque can go as far as I'm concerned. I didn't really feel we needed any of the illustrations.

I assume you'd be happy for parts of the text such as the breaks in the critical material to be very slightly reorganised to avoid wasting page space.

We should cut the footnotes as much as possible. I haven't done much work on these yet.

Other cuts. I know Arafat's poem is intended to be rubbish, but I think it slows the book down and just doesn't sit well in the text. So I've cut that. I've also cut odd paragraphs here and there that aren't needed. I'd also like to lose the letters that are largely non-English in content.

With the original *HOE #999* text, I feel that the odd really glaring typo should be corrected but overall I'm happy to leave the text as it is rather than attempting a full edit. As an example of a typo that should be corrected see page 15 of the current ms where 'MANES' can be replaced with 'MEANS' making the reading experience much smoother.

At some point someone will have to do a proper line edit, but let's get the text into a shape everyone is happy with first! There may be some issues Gavin or someone else has but we'll deal with them down the line if any arise.

You may also want to add some of the editorial correspondence to the book. I think the book ends nicely as it is, so if you want to add this, one way to do that would be as an appendix. But you may have a more creative solution to this matter. I think it would be a mistake to add all editorial correspondence, but again, we can worry about this and how to do an edit on them down the line…

Ciao, Stewart.

From: Jarett Kobek to Stewart Home, 23 November 2009

Hi Stewart,

For the vast majority of the edits—language changes, formatting changes—I am in complete agreement. I think there are one or two places where things might need to be changed back for technical reasons but otherwise no problems. Also was very pleased to see the image in the middle of the book suggested for cover or frontispiece—again, complete agreement. I've come up with a scheme for splitting the text into three sections as you suggest, which I'll incorporate in the next draft.

As for the footnotes, I like the idea of an acknowledgement page and its relative unobtrusiveness. There are, however, about ten to fifteen footnotes conveying specific information that I don't think can be incorporated anywhere else. My favourite example is the last footnote in the whole book, which explains the blood on the dance floor section of *HOE* and ties it to a specific instance in my life that can never be researched (attending a crummy concert). I'd like to keep these. I can go through and be very sparing with those that remain. If there are concerns about content (I know you found some too apologetic) I am more than happy to see if I can't tone down the *mea culpa*, such as it is. My guess is that once the footnotes that contain mere notation are removed, it'll make the remaining ones seem less obtrusive and also stop burying important info.

All of that said, my MAJOR concern right now is with the sections that were deleted. Namely Arafat Kazi's poem *Autoeroticism in the English Department*, the two letters in Bengali and the outsourced essay. I know you have been concerned about these sections from the very first draft—in particular Arafat's poem—but they serve a vital function. If the book's narrative pretext is that more than on third of it is written by people from the Indian subcontinent, it seems absolutely necessary to ensure that writing by people of its various ethnicities are present within the text. Other than communications from outsourcing companies, all writing by people of colour has been completely rewritten or deleted. Taken together with Mashruk's English, these communiqués demonstrate a limited tonal range varying between greed and incompetence. I am very, very uncomfortable with this and extremely concerned about putting a book into the world with my name on it that feels a little like a minstrel show done in brownface.

Each of the deleted sections (with the exception of the unedited outsourced essay, which I will deal with below) were picked for very specific purposes to achieve tonal broadening. Regarding Arafat's poem—*prima facie*, it seems like shit, but I think it also functions as a complete microcosm of the book. It really is writing done when he was twenty-one, its ambition wildly outpaces his ability, and it hits all the major themes. In particular, Arafat uses cross-cultural communication as a metaphor for the ambient angst and stupidity of the male mind in its immediate post-adolescence. This is *HOE #999*—the textfile and the book—in its entirety.

The letters in Bengali also emphasise this cross-cultural theme but in a radically different way. The first letter from Arafat to Mashruk is more formal, but I think helps anchor the narrative. The second letter, from Mashruk to Arafat, contains two things: Mashruk bitching about me and a meditation on Britpop, which I assure you is a very accurate depiction of how this type of conversation occurs in Dhaka. This latter part interests me considerably—it's a reflection of much of *HOE #999*'s content, which is, if nothing else, very, very concerned with pop music and its interpretations. I further find that these letters broaden the sense of the text existing within a world. I admit that some readers may well skip over them, but I think that for the readers who do stick them out, there's enough interspersed English to get a sense of what's happening. I absolutely do not want to lose these sections.

As for the first unedited outsourced essay, I'm far, far, far less attached to it than any of the other material. To be honest, I hate it, but I also feel like there is an energy that should be respected. I wonder if it would be possible to just include a very, very short excerpt—no more than 500 words. I can probably hack a limb off this Frankenstein's monster to provide both amusement and edification. But if there is adamant opposition to this presentation of the material, I'm certainly not going to waste my time trying to defend it. In summary: I'd like to keep something of it, but very, very little.

As I said at the beginning, I am happy with most of the edits. It's really just the issue of about ten to fifteen footnotes and the sections I've highlighted that give me pause. By and large everything seems close to done, so I'd like to work these out and see if I can't turn in a draft that'll be very close to final.

Thanks!

From: Stewart Home to Jarett Kobek, 23 November 2009

Hi Jarett,

My initial proposal was to use the first outsourced and not re-edited essay as an appendix rather than in the text itself. I didn't actually want to delete it because I think it is useful for people to see how bad it is. Gavin, however, preferred to delete it, whereas I wanted to move it and delete the letters you say are mainly in Bengali (and which Gavin liked much more than I did). In the end we reached a compromise at our end by deleting all this material.

The poem *is* utter shit. If this really has to go in, and I would much rather get rid of it than the first unedited outsourced text, then I absolutely don't think it should remain in the main body of the text but, might appear as an appendix. The overwhelming majority of readers will just think it is crap regardless of where it appears.

I have fewer problems with the letters, but I do think they're boring for non-Bengali speakers and will be skipped over by readers who don't know that language (although obviously there will be readers who are fluent in Bengali as well as English).

I'm not entirely convinced by your 'brownface' argument. As far as greed goes, doesn't that cut across cultural and geographical lines? Just look at bankers in London! Surely most readers will understand that capitalism is totalising and global; and also that race is not real, but is experienced as real because of racism. I feel the issue is dealt with from the off by the way you draw attention to the fact that those living in the overdeveloped world exploit those from outside it by, among many other things, outsourcing writing work and then taking credit for it. That said, while I'm not won over by your argument, it is your book and if you feel strongly about these points we'll include the material you want (absolutely against my better judgement in the case of the poem).

The intention of my edits is to make a good book better, but your rejection of some of them doesn't stop *HOE* being a good book—and since I enjoy a first-rate argument, for me the silver-lining to our disagreements is the way they'll create a lively end to the book (assuming we include them in an appendix)!

Ciao, Stewart.

*HOE #999: Decennial Analysis and Celebratory Appreciation,
or, The Dead Un-Dead*
Jarett Kobek
Semina No. 6
Published and distributed by Book Works, London

© Jarett Kobek, 2010

All rights reserved
No part of this publication can be reproduced, copied or transmitted
save with written permission from the publishers or in accordance
with the provisions of the Copyright Designs and Patents Act, 1988

ISBN 978 1 906012 21 2

Commissioning editor: Stewart Home
Edited by Stewart Home and Gavin Everall
Proofread by Gerrie van Noord
Designed by Fraser Muggeridge studio
Printed by Die Keure, Bruges

Book Works
19 Holywell Row
London
EC2A 4JB
www.bookworks.org.uk
tel: +44 (0)20 7247 2203

Book Works is funded by Arts Council England

HAHAHAHAH WHAT YOU MOTHERFUCKERS HAVE INVITED IS THE CRAZIEST NIGGA
THAT HAS EVER BEEN INVENTED

    I WANT TO SEE SOME BLOOD ON THE MOTHER FUCKING DANCE FLOOR

        i want to >SEE< some >BLOOD< on the
            motherfuckign DANCE FLOOR

    I WANNA see SOME blood ON the MOTHERFUCKING dance FLOOR

        i wanna see some BLOOD on the mnotherfuckign
        i wanna see soem blooD on the mother
i anwnwan see some bloord0krfjijsfjd on the mothetrufk
        ujafuabnwanjusgrj sese sometbl00d0
    njhamnefmotherufkernfhhfeuaeufea
        see soem bm00dl on the motherufkeirng
        some bseeing slf0b00dokwff mftoth
    sieiemgnmns lfsfopbl0fd0f0rfs mtotherufkcer
    ueksea0se0s0ef Bl00d0 thasaf eskmotharefklcuk
    see somet bomet0elrsajfuafheheajemgfmb
    ymefsmesoeollbe rbl00d motherufker see osme
        b0l0s0de son your
    monshthefsj,amfoiaefoae0f bl00d motherufker
    yeah v09l00b0slfdl vlofo0glerg omotehrufkcer
    al00vlersfj boalalae lb00d motherufker
        fuckienr g bm0therufblodo
        lb0b0b0lfer amotherufkcering
on fl0b00dkm blood0f0redkbld0r00roikfkf
        some0bl0d0f0lbmotherufkcer
        bl000d somemotherufkerbvlf0r0r
    olkfsl0bkwemfemotheruifkeingegk
soleemgogme4htingrs soledfasd mtheufking mbl00d
eiananfenepussy lb00d cug youtfgsacermbl0d00d
        bl00a0dlef on my mother0fkerufukign
    danmcieng fl00r0n blom0therufkb00dufkcerf
        lb00fslf0embl00djf0blbblamboozle[9]

---

[9]. On 16 November 1999, I saw Danzig/Samhain at Lupo's Heartbreak Hotel in Providence, Rhode Island. The opening band, a Nu-Metal act, was called either Cesspool or Crepuscular. The vocalist for the band repeatedly demanded his desire to see blood on the motherfucking dance floor. Thusly, my response.